Trident Arising

William Jewell Wadlington

PublishAmerica
Baltimore

ISBN: 978-1-4489-8578-4
PUBLISHED BY PUBLISHAMERICA, LLLP
www.publishamerica.com
Baltimore

Printed in the United States of America

DEDICATION

This book is dedicated to…

My wife, Janet, who has been my polar star for more than thirty wonderful years.

My daughter, Becca, who I pray will need to explain great-granddad's book to her grandchildren because they will not understand or have examples of bigotry and prejudice in their lives.

The undiscovered country.

"The mind of a bigot is like the pupil of the eye; the more light you pour upon it, the more it will contract."
—Oliver Wendell Holmes

FOREWORD

Bigotry and prejudice is a cancer that eats at the fabric of society. While Trident Arising is a fictional story, it is based on real occurrences in my life and set in real places. Since 911, the United States has become more security conscious and more focused on protecting our interest. Unfortunately, the United States governments and those who lead at the state, county and local level has not placed the same focus and deterrent for home-grown terrorism and bigotry. The bigots and racist who live among us are indeed using the complacency of good, average Americans to plan and to terrorize us all.

I have taken pains not to use racial slurs in this book because it advances hatred and acceptance. The fact that most readers will think of the names that are unwritten and unsaid is evidence enough for the change that is needed in this nation. As I write this forward, we have the fortune to have our first African-American president and there has never been the level of racial undercurrent present in the media, the coffee shops and bars.

Trident Arising is a warning, a testament to the average person who will dig in his heels and push back when needed and for true warriors who keep us free. Too many white supremacist and racist of other ilk are part of our armed forces; however, the true warriors and patriots abound and outshine any smudge or taint of the bigot. Trident Arising is a warning, as well, to the bigots, the racist, and the supremacist of all types. The warning will sound like a small voice in good times, but when forced to choose between bigotry and tolerance—will accept tolerance. The small voice will allow small, stupid people to make loud noises, but when pushed too far will arise and purge the bigot, the supremacist and racist and then go back to become the small, quiet voice that is America's conscience.

The people portrayed in Trident Arising are fictional, but are an amalgam of people who I have known. Many of the military personnel are representations of warriors who I served with in the United States Navy or that I have learned to respect from reading their works. Crew Twelve of Patrol Squadron Seventeen is not fictional and that group of warriors has been portrayed as the gentleman and patriots that they were and still remain. Unfortunately, the members of W.A.N. are also represents people who I known and been sorely disappointed in their beliefs. I have known bigots who hated for hate sake and who were much smaller I thought that a human being could become. I am disappointed in many of those whom I have known with small minds, weak intellect and misguided beliefs. My prayers count each one of them.

Finally Trident Arising is intended to be a quick, fast action, jump through the chapters. If you are frustrated that at a critical part of the action I chose to end that story and then pick it up again in two chapters, then I have done my job. I hope that you have as much fun reading Trident Arising as I had writing it—Enjoy!

TRIDENT ARISING

THE GENESIS—CHAPTER 1

Damn Yankees—Cumberland Church, Virginia
0930 Eastern Standard Time

For several days the Confederate troops had moved west toward Lynchburg via the rail head at Appomattox Junction. All the time the Federalist forces closed around the army of Virginia like a pincer. One of the ironies of war was that the last battle for the war would be fought in a place where the soil of the earth was already a blood red. It was almost as if the earth itself was bleeding because of this travesty and waste of human life. The Confederate troops fought with courage and hope as they moved from Farmville on April 7 to Cumberland Church and on west of the village of Appomattox. The numbers were far too uneven to hope for a retreat or a breakout. As one of the Generals of the battle later commented from his home in Indiana, "We were surrounded on five sides with the Yankees pushing for a sixth." Thankfully the commander of the surrounded army was a gentleman and a pragmatist.

The man clad in dirty confederate grey sat in the empty straw crib in the corner of the bombed barn. His rodent-like eyes continuously scanned for the slightest movement. The smell from the unkempt pile of decomposing manure would have driven any other man from his hiding place hours previously, but not this man. He could only smell the overwhelming influence of sulfur and cordite from the cannon he had manned as those chemicals wrecked havoc with his olfactory system. His blackened face and hands resembled the very people he fought to keep enslaved. He was a small man both in stature and in thought. His size often caused him to choose to abuse others who were of greater size or means. He was seen as a small man with a big problem.

His mind reeled with hundreds of images literally flooding his overloaded frontal cortex. The images of flashing bayonets and comrades with missing limbs would stay in his mind even when he shut his eyes tightly. The most poignant image was one of his battery commander pulling his severed leg behind him as he moved to the wrecked gun. The look in that man's eyes when he saw where the 'coward' Culliman had hid was an image that would haunt him for the rest of his life. The commander had released his leg and sank slowly to the earth. His accusing, dead eyes stared at the little man for a full ten minutes before he made his escape. Then, he stood, turned and ran with all his strength away from the battery commander's glare. He could feel the eyes on his back. He thought he even heard the dying battery commander yell at him, "Coward, damnable coward!"

He had hid and then ran. John and Julie Culliman's pride and joy had deserted his post and ran like a coward. How could he go home to Stone Mountain? They would all laugh. Even the slaves would snicker behind his back. But, what could be done now? He lapsed into utter zero thought. His mind became blank and he was at peace for the moment. The moment stretched into hours.

As he seemed near to falling asleep, the battery commander's eyes stared into his and he jolted wide awake.

The rebel rubbed his eyes with such intensity that he appeared to be attempting to wipe away the image.

The rebel weighed the possibilities and asked his inner self, "What now?" The sound of the question so illuminated his soul that he flinched and thought he had asked the question out loud.

As is with many rhetorical questions to oneself, the question was not answered by a vision or a divine intervention, but rather by an outside agency. A sound from outside that interrupted his focus and returned the feral rat to his mind. The rat was now chewing on his obdula oblongata; that portion of the brain where instinct is housed. The feral rat now chewed on the fight or flight response neurons. The corporal's survival center was fully engaged. Much like the gnawing rat, the small man became ready to run or to fight. He was poised, waiting, and ready.

The rebel quickly and quietly hid himself in the shadows and removed his Arkansas toothpick from the scabbard on his right hip. The knife had been given to him by his grandfather when he was ten years old. He looked at the brass hilt and the antler handle… "Stop!" his heart beat loudly in his head. "Focus!" hissed the rat. The sound became louder and now a shadow passing in front of the slats in the barn's walls. The rat continued to gnaw at Culliman's brain. As he hid, his face even mimicked the movements of the rat when seeking the next meal.

The door opened imperceptibly and a tall man quickly entered and moved into the darkness and stood very still. After the time it took for his eyes to adjust to the dark he moved along the stalls and settled on the ever present pile of straw. This newcomer was a different warrior in this battle against Northern aggression. The sound outside the barn turned out to be another confederate survivor. He was an educated man of high means. He had left his plantation in North Carolina when Jefferson Davis and Bob Lee made the first call to arms. After all he could not allow those Virginian snobs to get all of the glory.

Damn Yankees! They had taken his regiment and would probably take his leg if he didn't get this bleeding stopped. His pain forgotten for a moment, his thoughts turned to memories of his wife and two dear daughters. As quickly with memories, his thoughts turned to carnal thoughts of his wife. How on long, sultry afternoons he would lure his comely wife to the cool, inviting cellar and slowly remove all the many layers of clothing. He remembered, just like peeling an onion…

"What was that sound?" He crouched into a fighting stance. His senses were charged to the limit of their ability. He peered and heard more than he usually could.

A slight wheeze emitted from the corn crib opposite him.

He needed no urging to action. "I am Colonel Triplett of the Army of North Carolina. If you are Yankee, I will accept your surrender" said the tall confederate gentleman. This true son of the South was ready to give fight or accept surrender, but little else.

The silence enveloped the feral corporal like a blanket. He held his breath without knowing that his breathing had stopped. His heart threatened to leap from his chest and take on a life of its own. He was sure that the man in front of him could hear the blood pounding in his veins.

The cannoneer remained hidden and held his breath. The corporal had a vision of being hung as a coward or shot by this officer for running away. At times like this his genetic propensity for clear thought won out over his terror. His ancestors had passed on their genes by the survival trait of capitulation and deception.

Once again the Colonel spoke, "Come out now, by damn!"

Slowly the corporal leaned from his hiding place and caused his spine to take on a rigidness that was opposite to his nature. The rat gnawed away at the small man's brain. He finally decided to show himself. The rat smiled, "So it was going to be fight?"

"Sir, Corporal Robert Culliman of the Fourth Georgia Battery."

The Colonel automatically went into his commander mode. "Corporal, what are you doing here?" he queried. "Where is your regiment and who is your commander?" continued the Colonel.

The young corporal hung his head, but not in thought. This was part of the act.

Culliman responded, "Colonel…my battery was destroyed…all my comrades…gone… Why sir?"

The act had the desired effect. The colonel became the father figure. How many of his own men lay bleeding, dead, or captured. He had let those poor boys down; he had failed them. Sternly he said, "Soldier, focus on where we are now." He continued, "Neither one of us can bring back the dead." He finished his small speech by reassuring the corporal, "Corporal, stick with me and we will get back to our lines and make those Yankees pay with blood, by God!"

Bob Culliman allowed his head to rise slowly and inspect the Colonel better. He was a bit younger than him and slouched to his right side. His right hand tightly clamped his upper thigh. A dark spot stained the trouser leg. He also noticed the contorted face and saw the pain in the other's eyes. He thought to himself, "A walking dead man or at least a one-legged man." His conniving mind continued to review various scenarios. The rat was running free in his brain.

He quickly moved to the Colonel's side and helped him to sit in the previously used pile of straw. He helped the officer remove his blouse and made him comfortable. Each of these kindnesses were followed by a heartfelt, "Thank you, sir" from the Colonel.

Bob then set about the business of bandaging the leg. He ripped long swathes of cloth from the tail of his shirt. The tail was the only part of the shirt that wasn't black. After making the constricting knot as his grandmother had taught him, he pulled the knot as tightly as he could. The Colonel first winced, then moaned, and finally pulled himself away from the source of his pain.

"Sorry sir, but the knot needs to staunch the blood flow," said the Corporal.

As vision and breath returned to near normal levels, the Colonel spoke to the enlisted man, "That is quite all right, Corporal. I know that you have to tie that knot tight to stop my bleeding."

With this said Colonel Triplett closed his eyes and gave into the fatigue and the shock. Several times during his slumber his thoughts returned to the cool cellar and his lovely wife.

Then as if an icy bucket of water had been thrown into his face, he sat bolt upright. It took a moment for his mind and eyes to focus. He could not lift the weight from his chest and screamed from the pain in his chest. A stray thought passed through his mind, "Why can't I hear my own scream?" It was then that he felt the hand across his lips.

He sank slowly into unconsciousness and blissful death. Soon the pain would be over. His last cogent thought that flowed electron-by-electron out of the quickly oxygen-starving brain was, "My wife…my girls…"

The Meeting—White American Nation Compound near Bunker, Idaho
1930 Pacific Standard Time

The slap was rendered with such great force that the other man's head snapped back and blood began to flow steadily from both nose and mouth. Sam expanded his huge chest and began to prepare for the next act. Every muscle in his large frame was coiled and ready for release. Most humans have a 'fight or flight' reflex built into their psyche; Sam had only a fight reflex. The flight reflex had been whipped from him at an early age. He was ready to fight and eager to win.

The recipient of the slap turned and addressed his attacker through bleeding mouth, "Why the hell did you do that Sam? Damn it!"

Sam Becker was a large man who possessed quick reflexes and a trained ability to make instant judgment. His paternal grandfather had helped him with the latter. His grandfather had been a very old man when he took his brother Bob and he into the forest near their northern Georgia home and trained the boys in judgment. The judgment sessions still showed as scars that crisscrossed the back of his legs. His grandfather had told both him and his brother about the courageous Colonel and the failed mission to save Christendom. His great-great grandfather, he had been told, 'gave his all both during the *War of Northern Aggression* and afterwards'. The teachings of faith and judgment and mission had been a family tradition handed down from the Colonel to each boy child when the time came. The male children of the Becker line would be pointed spears at the heart of the non-whites and those who opposed white purity and a white America.

Sam addressed his bleeding colleague, "You used names to address the *INFERIORS*! You gave them worth."

His grandfather, who had been well tutored by his own father, had taught Sam. He only remembered his great-grandfather by association. He remembered the pictures of the small wrinkled man in the wheel chair and the sleeve pinned up to protect the missing arm. What he knew of his great-grandfather was told to him. The Colonel had been a true son of the South and a hero. He stood against his own troops and defied Robert E. Lee when he went to surrender in Virginia. From the teachings passed from father to son to grandson, Sam learned the real order of things. Virginians could not be trusted, all non-white, non-Protestants were not only non-Americans, but were inferior to the human race and did not deserve a name of their own. Sam could still here the catechism of his grandfather, "Only white Americans of Protestant faith are worthy. Inferiors deserve no name. God will protect those who rid the sons of Cain from His world. The road to righteousness is paved with cleansing the world of Inferiors." Both Sam and his brother Bob would recite this litany and then their grandfather would crisply bring the willow branches across their bare legs. He would then gather and hug the crying boys and tell them that the pain that they felt was caused by the Inferiors that infested their country. Both little boys would vow to remove that source of pain. Grandfather would smile and return to his reading.

The bleeding man wiped the blood from his mouth and addressed Sam, "I only said that we should be down in Spokane taking care of some of those spi…"

The word never made full enunciation in the mouth chamber as once again Sam's robust hand slapped the offender with open hand.

Every man has a limit and the slapped man had reached his. He turned on Sam and raised his fist to deliver a right cross. More quickly than one would expect from a man of Sam's size, he brushed the raised arm aside, pulled the man close by his shirt front, and effectively cut off the man's air with a Rangers' choke hold. The smaller man struggled and even slammed his fist into Sam's abdomen with no effect. He was quickly losing consciousness.

As the bleeding man's final struggle and choking noises began to dissipate, the leader of the service stopped and approached the pair. He did not hurry, but seemed to glide across the floor.

The Reverend Jim Stewardt spoke to Sam and his victim, "Brother Culliman, release Brother Clarke." He took both men by the hands and continued, "What is this about? We must not bicker among ourselves." Now the Reverend took on the persona of a kindly uncle.

The Reverend was a fiftyish, six feet tall man with a striking head of pearl-white hair. His square jaw and flashing teeth made him appear as one of those caring, Godly men who could as quickly turn into an avenging angel as a chameleon changes its colors. On several occasions exactly that happened. He had held a widow's hand in grief and turned and issued orders for a lynching or a burning. His handsome and charismatic demeanor belied the heart of an inquisitor/soldier of the fourteenth and fifteenth centuries in Spain. Jim Stewardt was a man others listened to and followed.

As neither man was of mind to speak, the Reverend gave instructions to his subordinates, "Sister Rosemarie, will you please see to Brother Clarke's injuries and determine the cause of this altercation." He released the injured man's hand but firmly held Sam's hand and when Brother Clarke and Sister Rosemarie had left earshot he turned and spoke to Sam, "Brother Culliman, we should speak of important things."

Sam and the Reverend moved through the 'church' toward the northwest corner. This building was the home of the White American Nation Church. It was far more a fortress than a church. The inner sanctum was a second wall of twin six inch rough-hewn logs with 1/4" sheets of Kevlar layered between. The Kevlar was expensive and had to be shipped as insulation, but the Reverend had well-to-do supporters in almost every state. The F.B.I. had a permanent observation site located a little more than a mile from the 'church'. He had had to take special precautions when his followers had constructed their home to make sure that secrets were kept from prying eyes. He smiled when he remembered the expression on the agent's face when he had Rosemarie take a thermos of hot coffee to the F.B.I. observation post. He wasn't sure if the coffee or the literature that he gave the agents infuriated them most. "Oh well." He thought, but God moves in mysterious ways.

As Sam and the Reverend approached the corner of the inner wall, both men looked around and pulled opposing curtains that overlapped behind them. The Kevlar and the water piping in the outer wall should decrease the likelihood of a thermal or I.R. imaging camera from prying into their sanctuary, but the lead curtain would surely prevent the prying eyes.

The Reverend tapped the top and bottom screw heads in the cover of a light switch that operated the track light system on the south and west walls. Each member of the inner sanctum had this code. As the final screw head of the seven digit code was fingered the light switch cover plate hinged to present an eight-symbol keypad. Seven of the contrived symbols represented numbers and the seventh functioned as an ENTER key. The Reverend looked to his left and Sam turned his back on the keypad while the reverend keyed in his code. When the reverend had finished his code he tapped Sam on the shoulder and the men reversed positions. When Sam had completed his six digit code and hit the enter key a distinct metal sound issued from the floor releasing the sections where the stairwell began. The floor sections slid easily and revealed another curtain at the base of a steep set of stairs. The pair proceeded down the stairs and through the curtain. As the reverend went through the curtain, he depressed a switch that caused the floor release mechanism to slide into their original position and firmly bolt shut.

An Officer and Gentleman—Cumberland Church, Virginia
1310 Eastern Standard Time

The confederate corporal lifted himself from the now-still body. His contemplative mind gave little quarter and little remorse. The dead man was nothing more than an opportunity for him. He started to plan how he would come home with his battlefield commission to full Colonel. That is the least he could do for his parents. A small smile crawled from corner to corner of his face as he thought how Sally Mae would come running to greet him as he passed the general store on his way to the saloon. He would show her father that he wasn't a worthless son of a stone farmer. That bastard would pay heavy when he saw the uniform and was heralded as a conquering hero. He might take Sally Mae directly to the preacher with a cheering group that pushed away the objections of a father. "Yes, what could he say with all of the cheering and backslapping?" he reasoned. For the time being the rat sat contentedly in the recesses of Colonel Culliman's mind awaiting the next time needed for survival.

The eyes are closest sense to the brain for a reason. He saw movement through a crack in the barn wall and his brain quickly moved his body to fight or flight mode…he approached the crack closer to see the full field adjacent to the barn. Across the field he saw three men moving with stealth and obvious fear toward the barn. He made a list of things he had to complete before the men arrived.

The newly promoted colonel stripped the owner of the former rank of all clothing. He dragged the body to a dark corner of the barn and covered it with the contents of the manure pile. He then sorted the useable clothing from the pile he formed by combining both the new addition and his previous clothing.

The former corporal moved to the barn again to check the progress of the three men heading toward the barn. He could now make out that they wore grey uniforms. Two of the number carried riffles with the bayonets still fixed to the muzzle. The third man carried a cannon ram that he used as a crutch. The trio was within 200 yards of the barn. He had to hurry.

Colonel Robert Culliman straightened his blouse and smoothed his hair. He had to look, and act, like an officer of the army of Georgia. He removed the 'NC' clasp from the blouse and threw them toward where the donor of this fine uniform lay with the other decomposing matter.

The trio of confederates was very close now. He could hear their ragged breathing and almost smell the fear they emitted in their flight from battle. "The COWARDS!" he thought. The newly emerged Colonel knew that he could recover these fallen comrades. They merely needed the direction of an officer.

Culliman moved the left of the door so that when the door was opened he would be behind the barn door. He straightened his scabbard and readied to greet **HIS** men.

Inner Sanctum—White American Nation Compound near Bunker, Idaho
2053 Pacific Standard Time
Whenever Sam came to the inner sanctum, he had a feeling of the switches hitting his bare legs. He could hear the litany and knew that he was closer to completing his mission and finishing what his great-grandfather could not than anyone before him. He was excited and focused. In a word he had the deadly combination of mission and method.

Reverend Stewardt spoke, "Sam, we must remember that not all of our comrades in this great battle are as refined and polished in our beliefs as we are." The charisma exuded like honey from a freshly broken honey comb. He continued, "We both have to remember that little children must be brought to the fold."

Several minutes passed as Sam weighed his response and reflected on the words spoken to him by his leader. He thought, "How this man was so much like my grandfather." Finally he spoke, "I apologize for interrupting the service and my quick response." It was an apology for the outcome, but not for the stand. "A good compromise was always a tactical advantage," he thought to himself and quickly moved to other pursuits.

The reverend smiled and spoke in a more direct manner, "Fine. Now where are we on the training of the raiders? We have…"

"You mean Stewardt's Raiders?" Sam interrupted the Reverend.

The Reverend smiled and thought to himself, "What a fine weapon I have in this young zealot." He would point Sam in the right direction and set him loose to remove the blight from his new country and to convert those who had lost their way. Sam would be a fine weapon indeed.

The Reverend continued, "We have to coordinate our plans and, of all of our plans, the raiders carry the most long-lasting burden for success of the plan."

"Stewardt's Raiders will be ready sir." Major Sam Becker continued, "Are we still a go on Trident in 10-days, sir?" Ten days and the mission would begin in earnest.

General Stewardt answered, "10-days and we liberate our brethren and establish our new nation of white pureness and Christianity."

Sam thought about how the plan had evolved and the sad realization that this revolution would be one that started with a few patriots. It might be years before the brainwashing and Inferior-based propaganda dissolve enough to continue to build their country.

The General had other thoughts. His were of the entire plan. He knew the weaknesses and the strengths. This would work and our brothers from throughout the world would join them. He opened the curtain that covered a white board. The Trident Plan was clearly listed:

TRIDENT—Prong 1:
1. Capture the National Guard armory at Coeur d'Alene.
2. Establish a front on the Pend d'Oreille River.
3. Establish a front at the crest of the Bitterroots.
4. Invade and encapsulate Spokane.
5. Establish a detention and reeducation facility in the liberated zone.
6. Assure the protection of the Heart of Columbia facility.

TRIDENT—Prong 2:
1. Secure the Kentucky.
2. Prepare for manual detonation.
3. Monitor and remain vigilant.

TRIDENT—Prong 3:
1. Liberate aircraft from M.H.A.F.B.
2. Hold M.H.A.F.B. and prevent resistance.
3. Attack Ecosafe.
4. Attack I.N.E.L.
5. Attack Upper Snake River Dams.

"What a glorious plan," the Reverend whispered.

Sam responded, "Our new nation, our ace in the hole, and our diversion. It will work sir. We will prevail." Sam smiled as his eyes moved back and forth across the battle plan. He actually licked his lips in anticipation.

"With God's help," the Reverend added. "Indeed, with His help and a few weapons," The Reverend mused. The Reverend placed his hand on the larger man's shoulder and squeezed gently as would a proud father. Sam responded like a son to this charismatic leader.

Command—Cumberland Church, Virginia
1740 Eastern Standard Time
"I say I saw someone looking out of that door," the tallest of the three whispered through his teeth. His eyes narrowed as he tried to see through the wood of the barn door.

The trio had found one another in a side channel to the main creek drainage to the rear of the main battle. All three men were in a state of shock from what they had witnessed. The youngster of the lot had a nail buried deep in his thigh and did not have the courage to allow either of the other two to even look at the wound. The nail came from a Yankee canon that had run low on standard issue ammunition or the gun crew just had a mean streak.

"You're mad! We need to get under cover. Come on!" the man with the corporal stripes proffered. The youngster with the leg wound was last to hobble to his feet and follow the lead of the corporal.

Cautiously the trio approached the door and eased it open just enough to peer inside. As the light from the fading sun poured into the dark interior, the young man using the cannon ram as a crutch pushed past the other two and stumbled, then fell on the straw floor near the corn crib. His fellows followed after their young comrade entered unmolested.

The three now sat near the corn crib and started to relax. It was as their eyes began to adjust to the gloom of the barn's interior that Colonel Robert Culliman of the Army of Georgia made his entrance.

As he stepped into the sunlight allowed by the partially opened door, he barked an order that every soldier since the days of the Roman Legions responds to immediately.

"Aaaa-Ten-Shun!" shouted the newly frocked Colonel. "This was going to be easy!" the feral rodent mind engaged again.

Had the would-be Colonel thought about what he was doing, he would have thought that officers never called attention themselves. This would be the first of several mistakes that the young Colonel would make that very afternoon.

To their credit all three men shot directly upright and presented themselves as real soldiers. "Sir, we did not see you…," the Corporal started.

The Colonel started his recruitment of **HIS** men. "Gentlemen, from this point on you have two duties to the Confederacy and your homes. The first is to protect me with your life." He looked from man to man and found that he would easily fleece these yokels in a poker game.

He continued, "The second is to follow my orders without question." He again scanned the faces and found no questions. He did not realize that each man had taken this oath before and the shock from the battle still controlled their emotions and judgment.

The second cardinal mistake made by the new Colonel was that he assumed that silence was the same as acquiescence. These men were survivors and had the 'roll-with-the-punch' mentality.

The young man was the first to interrupt the silence, "Sir, we are lost!" He continued with downcast eyes. My battery was destroyed and a rider came and told our officer that we were to 'cease all hostilities'. The rider continued and gave an order to the officer." The young man swallowed hard and continued his story, "The lieutenant told us that a cease fire had been declared and that General Lee and General Grant were on their way to Appomattox Courthouse to meet and discuss condition for surrender."

All four men now retreated into their own world. The young bearer of bad news openly sobbed while the older men began to slowly shake their head.

Culliman thought, "How could this be? Damn their eyes!" How could he be God's instrument when the cause was lost? That damned Virginian the man from Georgia thought. It is his fault. He was a Yankee officer before the great cause and will probably be one after. How can I stop this greatest of injustice? "Stop Lee!" the feral voice said. And since the feral voice controlled the mind, the body followed.

Colonel Culliman began, "You men have been chosen by God to perform…"

THE INCEPTION—CHAPTER 2

The Colonel—Holt's Junction (near Appomattox), Virginia
0530 Eastern Daylight Time

The Colonel and his men had slowly sorted their way from the barn that acted as shelter and command post to the bramble-infested hollow near the east-west road that ran to Appomattox Courthouse.

Colonel Culliman had commanded his men with all of the skill of an ignorant backwoods corporal, which, after all, is what he was. During his three years with the Fourth Georgia Battery he had few interactions with officers. His experience was following the commands of stout, bellowing sergeants. In fact his command style did not even reach that of a new sergeant. The saving grace in this lost command was that 'his' men were as ignorant and easily convinced by the uniform as was the newly appointed Colonel. Culliman thought to himself, "I was born to lead men."

One of his men groaned and passed gas loudly. Several others groaned. In the stillness of the woods this sounded like a bugle. The gnawing rat came to full alert in the Colonels brain and spoke with vim and vindictiveness to its host.

"The next man who makes a sound or movement to give away our position, I will kill personally," threatened Culliman. He turned quickly away from the men, not even making eye contact with each man to secure his threat. The uniform had not removed the mark of the rodent from his personality or bearing.

A light rain had fallen during the early morning hours and each man confined himself to shiver and maintenance of warmth. This could be one of the reasons for the bad tactical arrangement for the ambush.

The site was ideal. The wide road topped from a small creek and was bracketed on both sides with heavy woods with brambles. Horses would have difficulties scattering and expanding the killing zone. On the south side of the road a small hill rose three to four feet above the road. This hillside would be the ideal placement for snipers. The Colonel had not seen this possibility. Instead he had bunched his men in the hollow. Four working rifles rested in dirty hands had been procured on their night trek to this place. Each man had a fine rifled long gun and revolving horse pistol. Only one man knew how to load and operate the horse pistol, but quickly gave the others a crash course.

Tactically, Culliman could not have chosen a worse ambush location for his men. They were three feet lower than the level of the road and had only a narrow field of fire. If the ambush occurred too soon, the column would reverse its path and retreat to the creek bottom from where they had just passed. If the ambush occurred too late, a fast gallop would take the column out of their range in short order. This was not an ambush for men with brains and guns to return fire, but a hunting party for stupid animals. Culliman had always despised officers because they acted as if they were smarter and better than he and his friends. He would show those 'Gentlemen' how a real patriot took care of his land and made sure that traitors were dealt with immediately.

This road was chosen because it was one of four that approached the junction near the courthouse. He had chosen this road because it led from the heaviest fighting. His reasons were not sound, but he had a one chance in four that the accursed general would travel this path and he could single-handed cease this insanity about surrender.

A distance creak of saddle leather and the muffled snort of a horse brought each man to full alert. Someone was approaching the ambush. If Culliman had been a trained officer he would have posted a lookout to signal if their desired targets were nearing their fate, but this too was beyond the gentleman from Georgia.

The sound of horses crashing through the nearby creek caused the guns to rise to level and the hammers to be cocked. Each man knew that his destiny was at hand. The tension was as thick as the mud that was slowly moving into the men's garments.

Suddenly the sound of a galloping horse caused the four ambushers to tighten their attention and several to tighten their trigger fingers.

Culliman swore, "Damn!" as the percussion and deafening roar of a long rifle exploded in his ear. His natural reflex was to fire as well. His finger pulled the trigger again and again. His terror was so great that he forgot that he had only a single shot to fire.

The smoke was heavy before them. A horse whinnied and men shouted. He lost sight of his men, the column and everything else beyond several feet. The smell of gunpowder was heavy in the depression and firing erupted from every corner. Now he heard orders being barked and groaning coming from close by. The sound of a pistol being discharged rang through the smoke covered scene from hell.

Culliman asked no one present in a voice only heard within the confines of his own head, "What happened?"

The next few minutes would tell. He grabbed his horse pistol. His eyes narrowed as he looked through the swirling smoke and saw the horse and rider on the ground in the opening, but something was wrong. This man didn't have the broad brim hat, but a billed campaign hat. His mind did not register the difference on the hat and the man on the ground. His mind asked, "What is the meaning of that hat?" No answer was immediately forthcoming. No, it could not be. He raised his horse pistol to continue the volley, but he could not make his finger pull the trigger. "Strange, this was not right," he thought as he heard the blood pound behind his eyes. Again the self-appointed Colonel said, "Strange?"

The General—White American Nation Compound Near Bunker, Idaho

2130 Pacific Standard Time

The war cabinet was assembled in the concealed operations room of the bunker. Each man had the rank of major. There were no colonels in this Army of Columbia. A clear separation between the commanding general and leader and his officers were required.

When the leader spoke it was with authority with no questions and a clear opening in the chain of command that allowed no questions and simple loyalty. Each major had his assignment that would be carried out with clear and efficient ease. The leader had made sure that each of his majors only had to complete one task and not be burdened with how other efforts were fairing.

Reverend Stewardt began, "Gentlemen, Trident will begin tomorrow night."

This said, he allowed a long time for that statement to sink in. He had learned at Seminary that the pause wrapped the message like a cloak. It protected the message and assured the speaker of total control. Every eye was glued to him and his words would hold complete and utter meaning.

As he scanned the table, he again thanked the Lord God for these men. They would be the instruments to do his will.

In addition to the 'General', eight men sat at the table. Six majors were present for Trident Prong One—the Establishment of Columbia. One major each would suffice for Trident Prong Two and Three.

The one major that would strike the first blow and had the best trained men was Major Sam Becker. The other majors had greater fronts and a greater strategic authority, but Sam would be his weapon—his sword of Gideon.

The leader began his sermon after the poignant pause, "We will begin Prong One immediately." He placed his hands on his hips and said, "All mighty God, thy will be done."

Armory—Coeur d'Alene, Idaho
2300 Pacific Standard Time

The Sheriff's car was ablaze across the street. A single shot stilled the crawling form that now lay silent on the asphalt. "It was their poor timing that caused them to die. This was a war and war had casualties," the marksman thought from his perch. He had no concerns or remorse for what he had just done.

The major arrived next to the sentry and said, "Ten minutes Jake and we will be gone." He further asked, "What does Rover report?" The 'Rover' team was a special unit to remove response to Trident One by removing infrastructure and key personnel. Rover was working with laser-like precision. Planning had been raised to an art form and the dividends were seen in the results.

"Major, Rover said that they have control of the emergency response center and the fire station that got the call. Rover said that they have twenty three NWBCs," continued the sentry.

The Major smiled. His was the first unit to report Non White Body Counts to the Reverend. "Jake, tell them well done and to follow the plan. No free lancing. We will all get our chance to cleanse our Nation."

Suddenly Jake placed his middle finger to his left ear and bent his head. His head raised and he addressed the Major, "Sir, we have another Sheriff's car heading our way."

The Major said, "You know what to do." After saying this, the Major returned to the armory to oversee loading and to light a fire under some asses.

The sentry moved into the shadows and waited. The Sheriff's S.U.V. rounded the corner and stopped eighty meters from his hiding place. The sentry aimed his grenade launcher at the darkness between the ground and the bottom of the S.U.V. He thought to himself about how television shows always had grenades launched into a vehicle's interior. No, the best place is just under the rig next to the gas tack. The swoosh sound of the rocket-propelled grenade surprised him. He opened his eyes just in time to see the Bronco elevated from the ground. Several rounds pinged off the dumpster next to him. The officer had survived the grenade attack and was shooting in the direction of the grenade plume. The sentry keyed his mike, "Eagle Eye, do you have a target?"

"Sentry, this is Eagle Eye. Roger. Stand by." Eagle Eye took a short breath, made correction for the downward angle, and squeezed slowly against the trigger. Eagle Eye hated the silencer. "Half of the reason to shoot was to hear the sound of a butt load of powder sending death through a hollowed-out piece of steel. Oh well." he thought. Killing was killing.

The shot took the deputy right between the shoulder blades. His gunny had told Eagle Eye that to hit a man in the spine between his shoulder blades and death was instant. Eagle Eye had been a good student. The police officer lay still while the expanding shadow of his spilled blood followed the path that gravity dictated.

Eagle Eye clicked his mike once. This was a signal that the target had been eliminated. Eagle Eye returned to his seat in the contrived balloon basket. It had been his idea to rig the three surplus weather balloons together, fill them with helium and raise them to 50 meters on a tether. There were no tall buildings near the armory, so his perch was a great sniping platform. He looked to the side of his basket at the 50-caliber sniper rifle. He probably would not get to use her tonight. Eagle Eye apologized to his lover, "Sorry sweetheart, no rock-n-roll tonight. But soon, O yes! Soon!" he slowly rubbed his Remington 30-06 with the soft towel and spoke to her, "Nice job baby, right where I put the cross." His face took on rapture as he said, "Beautiful!"

The sentry and Eagle Eye heard three clicks in their ear set at the same time. This was the signal that the goods were ready to be secured and moved to the compound. Eagle Eye saw Rover and his six vehicles move in front of the convoy. He watched through his night vision scope as Sentry loaded in the last truck and the disappeared up Government Way to the North. Eagle Eye was finished as soon as the sentry left his vision. It was time for the eagle to fly, or land in this case. He thought to himself how this balloon idea seemed stupid to him when first described. As he began to accept the plan, he calculated his odds at 50-50 to get out of this alive. He shook his head as he thought of how easy it had all been. How could their cause fail?

Eagle Eye pulled the yellow line and one of the three balloons began to leak. At the same time he started to reel the down rigger reel that tethered him to the ground. As he came to rest on the ground he pulled the green and the blue cord releasing the remaining gas. In ten minutes he had placed the entire balloon rig in the storage shed and loaded his two rifles in his pickup. He returned to the house and kissed his mother good bye. She was sleeping on the couch. He, then, went to his father's room. The man, old before his age, lay with a breathing tube sticking from his throat. He was slowly dying. It had been ten years since that drunken non-white had ended his father's life. He kissed his father on the forehead and said, "I will make them pay in full, Dad! One will die for every second you have suffered." Eagle Eye pledged as a tear rolled down his cheek. Yes, they would pay with blood and life. One at a time. He turned toward the door, wiped his eyes, and gritted his teeth.

Eagle Eye got into his truck and started West on I-90. As he did so, he inventoried his ammunition in his mind, "500 rounds of 50 cal., 200 rounds 30-06, 100 rounds armor piercing 50 cal. That should raise quite a ruckus!" Eagle Eye was almost giddy. He whistled a favorite tune and reflected about the surprise that his friends would have when they awakened to the new world that he helped create.

The blood from the deputy shot between the shoulder blades made a splattering sound as it dripped into the storm drain. Little other noise could be heard except the crackling of the two vehicles still burning softly. Coeur d'Alene was once again peaceful.

The convoy of trucks liberated by Eagle Eye was a fine start to fully arming an army of 500 men, but that was only one reason to take the armory. In reality, the six trucks only added 5% to the stockpile arms at the compound and in nearby caches. This was the only real quantity of arms for citizens with desire to revolt. That option was now removed. Eagle Eye had completed his first mission with distinction.

The Raid—Mountain Home Air Force Base, Idaho
0130 Pacific Standard Time

A sneeze erupted to his right. "Damn," he thought, "must be the fly-fly boy." He thought to himself about what they had to do this night. Invade an Air Force base, steal two F-111's, and then destroy any hope of immediate retaliation. Another sneeze made the night come alive like someone pounding on a bell. "Must be the sagebrush, some people just couldn't tolerate the pungent plant," the commander speculated.

Everything had changed after September 11. The change was not good for Trident, but this world was the one he had. He had thirty good, well-trained, hard men under his command. They were a weapon ready to be unsheathed and deployed. Now was the time and Mountain Home was the place.

Mountain Home Air Force Base lay in the southern Idaho desert. Sagebrush, Greasewood, and Rubber Rabbit brush were the predominant native plants; however, when man applied water to this arid land, it bloomed into incredible richness. The land to the west was some of the finest farm land in the world. The base was isolated and considered secure from attack both domestic and foreign. The authors of that statement were clearly becoming wrong and mislead when they surveyed what they considered a wasteland.

A crackle in his earpiece then a whisper, "Sensor lines tricked." The commander grinned at this news. It meant that his electronics had been spliced into the remote sensor and an 'all clear' message was continually being fed to the control center. The bored guard would see no difference until well after it was too late to do anything about it. He clicked his transmit button twice. This was the signal to move forward. He did not hear the men to his left or right, but could sense them moving through the sage.

As he crawled over a small rise, his pulse raced. "There they are!" his mind whispered. The intelligence report was correct. Two F-111Bs in a hanger, armed to the teeth and ready to rumble. He was told that the venerable old fighter aircraft were kept for the general of this base. A superstition that an attack would come and his other 'ready aircraft would not be ready'. This folly would cost them dearly.

Mountain Home Air Force Base occupied a great deal of sandy soil, sagebrush, and little else. The base was considered safe because it was so large and the air field operations were miles from any road. Even before 9-11, the base was secure because of the single road that led from the interstate and the three concentric rings of overlapping security. The first ring of security was a twelve foot high fence that encircled the entire base. While the original design called for trembler sensors on the fence that soon was disconnected because of the animal activity. The guards soon found that jack rabbits and even pocket gophers set off the alarm.

The second ring of security was a buried motion sensor system. The sensor elements had an effective lateral range of fifty meters; however, the flaw was that they required another sensor to create the 'breakable' field. His second had just eliminated that threat to detection.

The final ring of security consisted of no less than twenty overlapping Air Police patrols. The patrols overlapped into the flight line and into the base proper. Half of the patrols were mounted on bicycle or truck; the other half on foot. Each trained A.P. had an M-16, side arm, and smoke/flare canister. Each guard was also wired. Central Security constantly monitored open mikes on the guards. The Mountain Home invaders knew the details of security because the Major in charge of security made sure that they knew. He was one of thousands of 'True Americans'. The major was a Colonel in the White Army of North America.

The commander keyed his mike again. Three clicks this time. Slowly his command deployed. He could hear the soft rustle of fabric against sage brush. A hand grabbed his ankle and he almost reacted. It was one of the fly-fly boys. Just before the man spoke, the commander covered his mouth with his hand. He made the universal sign to be quiet by placing his index finger perpendicular to his lips. He, then, pointed both fingers to his own eyes then pointed to the aircraft. The fly-fly boy smiled. Then he pointed to the flier and into the darkness to his left and clenched his fist. This was a signal for the fliers to stay put and wait. The flier nodded and gave the thumbs up symbol. "Probably something he got from watching Top Gun," thought the commander.

A muzzle flash at ten o'clock position, the commander was alert and pressing his night sight toward that direction. "Good, it has begun." Two more muzzle flashes to his right. No alarm yet.

Loss—Holt's Junction (near Appomattox), Virginia
0550 Eastern Daylight Time

The self-appointed Colonel slowly sank to his needs and looked to his right elbow. He again tried to pull the trigger of the horse pistol in his right hand. It was then that his eyes widened and panic began to take over his senses. The pistol was gone. He started to retrace his steps to find the dropped pistol. It was not a logical thing to do, but his mind was not bent on logic. Culliman was sinking into the oblivion of shock. "There it is," the former corporal said in his own mind. The pistol lay in a shallow hole. It was clean and looked ready to perform its deadly task. Culliman reached down with his right hand to retrieve the pistol. "No!" the words first exploded from his lips, then continued with a hiss as the gravity of the situation assaulted his senses.

Culliman wanted to look away, but he could not. Blood was dripping from his lower arm and his sleeve had a black glossy appearance. But the most horrific part of the scene was his thumb. His thumb was on the wrong side. "How could that be?" He mused. Suddenly the smoke and vegetation blended together in his sight and darkness began to invade from the sides of his vision. His fall continued until his right shoulder hit the ground, and then a thunderclap of pain. The little corporal from Georgia gently slipped into unconsciousness and dreamed of being home. The rat stopped gnawing at his brain and went back into the recess where it would again emerge when needed.

Lucinda was her name and they were sixteen together. He drifted along the muddy bottom creek near Stone Mountain following Lucinda. He crouched behind the bush as she slowly removed her clothes before the pool. He thought to himself "I need a better view." As he tried to move, a branch grabbed his right arm and held tightly. He pulled, but the pain became searing. He had to get away. The bush was keeping him from seeing Lucinda before she slipped into the pool. He tugged with all his strength, but suddenly could not feel his hand. Now the bushes, Lucinda, and the creek were gone. In its place a scene he could not identify. "What! Who was screaming? What was that terrible smell?" his mind thought as he slowly moved back toward consciousness. His eyes fluttered open. He saw the blue sky with whiffs of smoke moving across his vision. He then saw the face of the man splattered in blood standing at his side. His mind focused for just a moment, the rat began to awaken, then blessed darkness.

Boomer—Bangor Submarine Base near Keystone, Washington
0430 Pacific Standard Time

The SSBN Kentucky lay at berth at the Bangor Submarine Base. The 'BN' in the designator referred to the fact that this huge ship was a Nuclear, Ballistic submarine. It had the more common designation by friend and foe—BOOMER. High security surrounded the craft in the current war footing. Even though the Kentucky was off deployment and undergoing scheduled maintenance and re-supply, the submarine was a beehive of activity. Each of the MRV-ballistic missiles required refueling, testing and maintenance. The Multiple Warhead Re-entry Vehicle platform was a tricky piece of technology that required training and a top secret clearance. It was a sad fact that highly intelligent, highly trained men and women could give into hate and intolerance, but a truism. Even on a state-of-the-art Ballistic Missile Submarine of the most powerful Navy on Earth. The best and most thorough background check could not identify bigotry, hatred, and prejudice. Perhaps some day, a background check would not be necessary.

The First Class Missile Technician glanced at his watch for the fiftieth time in the past two minutes. He would show the people back home. He had begun his training as a racist in a Subic City Bar in Philippines. He and others of his race had liberated a bar for whites only and planted the Confederate Battle flag at the entrance. This in itself would probably not have been of issue, but when they sat at the front door and harassed their fellows, they crossed the line.

The missile technician looked at his watch again. He waited but a minute and checked his watch again and made sure that he knew where every other person in the compartment was standing. Sweat beaded on his forehead at a rate inversely proportional to the slowly reducing time left until he had to act. As he waited for the seconds to slowly tick to the desired time, his thoughts turned to an earlier incident that would form his attitudes for the rest of his life. Like many other human beings, his defining moment was a violent time and traumatic in its nature. He remembered a time in Philippines.

At first his compatriots in the Aryan Brotherhood Bar had success. However, that changed when the flight crew from a P-3 Orion strolled by. Never in his wildest dream did he believe that white men would side with a non-white. His dreams were about to be shattered. They had harassed the black man on the crew and invited the whites to join them. This was their first mistake.

The second mistake quickly followed. They judged that when the Bar crew approached the black aircrewman, the whites of the crew would back off. They did not. In fact they quickly moved shoulder to shoulder with their fellow aircrewmen.

The third mistake that they made was not to take notice of the size of the individuals in this crew. Each wore a ball cap that said VP-17, Crew Twelve. The smallest of the crew was 200 pounds and the twin large men pegged the scales at 240 pounds. Their patrol plain commander boasted that he tossed more beef on his plane than most steak houses did on a good Saturday night. The individuals from Crew Twelve were calm and gentle men, but when enraged offered more than they received. It only took twenty-five seconds for the scuffle to be finished. The eight aircrewmen remained standing while the fifteen Aryan Brothers collected lost teeth, nursed knuckle bumps, and limped away on sprained or broken limbs. Crew Twelve stood shoulder-to-shoulder and made no comment. Their solemn silence said what their fist had recently preached.

The First Class checked his watch and said to himself, "It's time!"

He heard the sound of shouts and scuffling and quickly brought the hidden pistol into view. He slammed the control room hatch and leveled his pistol at his fellow compartment mates.

"Line up against that bulkhead, now!" he barked. He was entering his time and his training with White American Nation was kicking in. He felt calm; a surge of righteousness coursed through him like an electrical current.

The men in the missile compartment looked surprised, but slowly followed the command. The barrel end of the pistol appeared to be the size of a sewer pipe when pointed at your head. Each man had undergone training for this kind of possibility, but the rules changed when the invader was a member of the crew. One missile man who had reluctantly moved to the bulkhead started to speak and earned a pistol across the check. The blood flowed with a red flourish. The first Class Missile Technician smiled. He thought, "Now, I'm in command."

Again the First Class Missile Technician spoke, "All of you keep your hands on the bulkhead or I will kill you. No sound. Eyes forward." All of the men complied, but continued to sneak glances over their shoulders when they could. Navy training provided some defensive fighting technique and several of the men had some martial arts training.

"They would pay," the First Class Missile Technician thought. He still had the scars and embarrassment of the beating by the hands of that large black man from crew twelve. "Yes they would pay; all of them; damned aircrewmen anyway. They would pay." His focus changed to center on his revenge.

The first class walked behind each man and made sure that each had no weapons. As he passed by Washington, he raised the pistol barrel and calmly shot a hole in the back of his head. He was just like that one in Subic City. The man was dead before his blood splattered the bulkhead or his body hit the deck. For just a moment the concussion from the shot made him focus on the bulkhead. His ears rang a bit.

"One less to kill later," he said out loud without knowing he spoke.

He then saw movement. It was the kid from over the mountains.

The first class remembered talking to this kid. He said he was from a small town in Central Washington called Peshastin. The kid spoke with a smile on his lips as he described frosty fall Friday nights at Peshastin Field playing football. What did he say his school's mascot's name was? Oh, yeah, Kodiaks. "Were there Kodiaks, Big-assed Grizzlies, in Washington State?" he wondered. The kid said that he loved to hit a guy in an open field tackle.

He swung his pistol, but too late. He was plucked from the standing position and lifted to end across the deck in a crash. His pistol flew from his grip and his body was raked with pain from a perfectly executed tackle. The former Cascade Kodiak grabbed this mutineer by the front of the shirt and began to pound with all his might and rage. Coach had told him to finish the tackle. That's what he planned to do.

The first class lay on his back and did not yet comprehend this attack. Somewhere in his mind a voice had started to count the blows: 16, 17…" Then all was calm and he fell into a deep hole. His revenge was over. He continued to fall.

Now the men in the missile room moved to action. They turned as one man when the hatch to the central corridor began to swing open. Men on both sides of the hatch moved quickly, but one group clearly took control of the hatch.

CONDITIONS OF CONFEDERATION—CHAPTER 3

Judges 15:16—White American Nation Compound (near Bunker, Idaho)
0300 Pacific Standard Time

The Reverend paced about his compound. He was agitated and when he was agitated, he mumbled to himself. Usually the mumbling was in the form of one of the Psalms or a favorite passage. He was now quoting from Judges 15:16. "...and the Philistines were smote with the Jawbone of an ass." He continued to pace.

His men eliminating the godless agents that were posted outside his compound would soon fracture the quiet of the evening. As he spoke, a squad of his best was aiming their night-scoped sniper rifles at the agents. The plan was working just as planned. They knew the routine, had recorded the communication between the agents and their base, and they understood the enemy—completely. He would soon become safe within the Trident zone.

The reverend suddenly fell to his knees and began to pray for strength and the guidance of the Lord in his heaven-sent mission. He thought he heard several snaps, but that could not be. Some of his riflemen were close to one-quarter mile away. Some of his faithful would be taking the place of the dead agents to insure that any visual check of the agents would insure operations as normal. The sound happened again. This time a movement of air caused him to end his reverie and turn to look behind him.

The reverend looked up into the man's face. He saw a smile and a look of self-satisfaction on the man's face. His lieutenant spoke,

40

"General, we have secured the compound and have complete control of the ground and airspace for twenty-five miles in all directions." The Reverend, now General, returned to complete his prayer. Just as rapidly as he fell to his knees, he rose from the floor. He turned and his face became grim and clouded as he became the General of the Army of the White American Nation. The change was not lost on those around him.

"How long until we get confirmation on Trident One and Two?" he asked his communications officer as he strode into the war room.

"Trident One reports and confirms being engaged," said the communications officer. The Comm. Officer continued, "Trident Two is engaged and Trident Three is Operational."

The General looked long at the wall with the masterstrokes written in three parts of the Northwest. He thought to himself, "It is time." The Reverend turned General exhaled meaningfully and seemed to become larger in stature as his plan, his dreams, came to pass.

In contrast to the revolution and excitement in the compound, the forest outside was quiet and calm. The rustling of pine needle detritus could be heard as the red-backed vole foraged for his meal. Without warning, the Snowy owl swept from the sky and snatched the vole in its talons. Like a sleeping America, the vole never heard the owl's approach. And like the vole, America would be unable to react with the quickness and ferocity needed to escape the coming of the killer.

High Ground—Spokane, Washington
0523 Pacific Standard Time

The advance Scouts had just finished gathering their gear and pulling the handles out of their rolling duffel bags. Each man carried either on his person or in his bag a small arsenal. In fact as the lead scout had pointed out on their drive in from North Idaho, each man had firepower equal to an entire squad that stormed the beaches on D-Day in World War II.

The drive to Spokane had been uneventful. Each man among this assault group wondered and contemplated where the invasion would occur. This squad of the faithful did not have information about the other operations. This group was to disrupt and provide distraction and cover for the main advance. Each man knew that their chances of surviving the assault were small, but each had lived through other do-or-die missions. "Anyway, we are in service of our brothers and sisters," mused each in his own time.

Spokane was a sprawling city located in a river valley. Interstate 90 bisected the town north and south. Most of the major businesses were located between the interstate and the river. Division Street divided the town east and west. The layout of the city, while not planned, was perfect for a small group of riflemen to bring travel to a stop. As this group of highly trained and qualified snipers traveled to their destination, Spokane awakened and started to begin the business of the day. I-90 was full, Division Street had bumper-to-bumper traffic; however, there was not the usual honking of horns and other distractions that usually are coupled with the commute in other cities. The drivers in Spokane loved living in this area and appeared to have just a little more patience than those from the other side of the state.

The high rise was an old gothic style building with a flat roof and external fire escape stairs. An aging elevator and an auxiliary elevator served it. Someone in the building had decided to place potted trees on several of the upper levels of the building providing an even greater illusion of the truly gothic. It was perhaps a bit ironic that even in this urban setting, each man could still take cover behind a tree.

The four men rolled through the lobby and proceeded to the elevator. One man went down the two flights of stairs to the mechanical room. His would be the trickiest portion of this mission. They conducted a dry run several days prior and rode the elevator ten times or more. Each time they calculated the greatest time needed to reach the roof and secure the elevator. He hoped that their calculations were correct.

The other three members of the Scouts had arrived at the level below the roof. One of their numbers began to work on the door that provided access to the roof and the others placed small charges at the stairwell entrance and the external fire escape entrance. In addition to these specifically placed charges, additional general charges were placed on the top of the panels of the false ceiling. Each charge was pre-numbered and specially designed to provide the greatest effect for any given location.

As Scout Three completed his final explosive, he reviewed how he had designed the small powerful explosives in a soda can with nails surrounding the explosive interlaced with phosphorus from road flares. He thought, "Whoever is on the receiving end of that party favor will be the best advertisement for DO NOT DISTURB!" After installing the explosives, the two Scouts began to install two tiny cameras at floor level. One at each end of the hall would provide the best possible warning system. They had reviewed a number of options: infrared cameras, ultraviolet detectors, motion sensors, even olfactory sensors. How the hell would they smell them coming? They had chosen a small pencil video camera with a wireless transmitter. They had exploded several of their charges next to the cameras and they worked well enough to see movement even when extremely smoky.

A sharp rip of steel was the indication that the third scout had gained access to the roof. The three scouts began to work their way up to the roof and set up the defensive and sniper positions. One of the disturbing elements of this location was the two buildings within shot range that had elevation on the building. This was disturbing because they could easily fall prey to a sniper bullet from one of those buildings. While this was of concern, each man also knew of the precautions positioned on the roof of each of the buildings in question.

Scout One unloaded his duffle quietly and with practiced efficiency. He was proud of his arsenal and the deadly efficiency that each weapon would soon reap. While he loved the M-107 50-caliber sniper rifle, he looked forward to the destruction he would cause when he sent the rounds from the 60mm Light Mortar to their targets. He thought as he scanned the wakening city, "What a wake-up that will be for this quiet little town."

A sound came from the rooftop door. All three of the scouts turned as one man to face the threat. Their Alliant XM8 assault rifle had a 100-round double drums magazine and could easily deliver all one-hundred rounds in less than 10 seconds. Scout Four slowly pushed his hand with a thumbs-up signal through the doorway, and then slowly stepped on to the roof. The other scouts slung their rifles on their back and moved to the doorway. Two scouts reset the steel door in its jam; while the third took out the tube filled with the iron oxide, ground aluminum and potassium permanganate. The tubes were positioned around the intersection of the door and the jam. Insuring that the end of the hollow tube that ran throughout encasing tub remained available; all three scouts placed the ceramic-backed tape over the entire jam-door interface and secured it with duct tape. A sudden low rumble came from the building beneath their feet and the fans ceased their motion in the exhaust vents adjacent to the door. Scout Four smiled while he was setting up for the next stage of the operation.

Broken Arrow—Submarine Base near Keystone, Washington
0445 Pacific Standard Time

A pistol was shoved through the hatch opening from the corridor side and five rapid shots pounded the deck, overhead, and bulkheads. The shots ended when the same kid who had tackled the mutineer put his technique against the hatch. A scream erupted from the corridor, the pistol fell to the deck, and the hatch was sealed and dogged.

The section leader, a newly frocked Lieutenant Junior Grade, ordered the men into the battery room that led to the engine spaces. The section leader said, "You men go into the battery room, secure and dog that hatch. Then get the welder and weld the seam of the door. There is an arc welder in the engine space." Several men began to speak, but he quickly raised his hand to silent them. The section leader continued, "This hatch is vulnerable. They are rigging a come-along, or hydraulic ram to open this hatch. I will hold them off as long as I can. It should give you the time to get the secure hatch sealed into the battery compartment."

As the sounds from the hatch increased, he heard the cackling of an arc welder on the battery room hatch. He never had imagined that he would be in this type of predicament. He was just a guy from Idaho who loved engineering. He never imagined that he would be repelling borders on a nuclear submarine when he was in sitting in his classroom at the University of Idaho. He heard the strain being placed on the hatch leading to the mutineers and then heard a 'clunk' sound through the bulkhead, "Good!" the Lt. J.G. thought, "The chain that the mutineers were using to try to get into his compartment had failed." He was scanning around the compartment trying to discover some help from the materials at hand. He heard the sound of the chain re-engaging the hatch and heard a hinge buckle under the strain. It was only a matter of time before the hatch failed.

The J.G. picked up the pistol and looked at the spanner wrench that jammed the hatch mechanism closed. Then he heard the rustling of chains against metal even louder than before. He poised the pistol at his best guess of where the crack would appear.

Home—Stone Mountain, Georgia
1252 Eastern Daylight Time
For the third time that morning he had scratched the scab on the healing limb. The pain made him angry and frightened at the same time. The Colonel had received the best treatment that the Federalist surgeons could provide, even though the man was the enemy. The doctor had dipped his recently amputated stump in Tincture of Iodine twice a day when bandages were replaced. His screams and cursing only made the doctor more convinced that he was doing the right thing. Then the stump was liberally coated with Carbolic Acid and wrapped tightly with clean, boiled linen. When the carbolic acid was sprinkled

on the wound, it would react and actually get warm enough to put off a small amount of vapor. This reaction was probably due to impurities in the tincture. His young surgeon spoke of disinfecting the wound to remove the possibility of infection, but he just thought that those bastards were torturing him in new and different ways.

Culliman had spent seven weeks in the hospital and in the recovery camp. He was surprised to discover that he was not a prisoner of war. Robert E. Lee had surrendered and the remainder of the armies of the Confederacy shortly thereafter. "We have lost." he thought. He hated that damn Virginian for his treachery. How could we keep on going with so many lost for nothing? To think that he had lost his arm to another Confederate Officer on the last day of the war, it made him cry.

He had been questioned in the weeks after surgery about his part in the attack. The Major had told him what transpired. The Major said," Colonel, sir, we were under a white flag of truce escorting General Lee to a meeting with General Grant." The Major continued, "Your men came out of the brambles and fired into the column. Thankfully only a Yankee Captain was grazed in the arm and a horse was killed."

Culliman stopped the Major there and asked, "Major who shot my men and did this to me?" As he spoke, he grimaced away the pain and lifted up the stump of his right arm.

The Major looked away and paused. With a bit of a catch in his voice he addressed his superior officer, "Sir, I inflected that wound." Culliman looked into the eyes of this man and could not fathom why a fellow son of the South would attack him. Culliman looked away first and turned his back on the man. As the man walked away Culliman mumbled to himself, "Traitor, damn traitor."

Bob Culliman was approaching the center of town when he was first spotted. He looked up the road and saw people start to walk into the street and stare. Other people leaned out windows. He wanted to run away. Would they believe the field promotion story as easily as the

Yankee Lieutenant did? His knees were wobbling a bit. He had not eaten that day. He was hot in the wool uniform blouse. His right sleeve was pinned up to his shoulder. He had $31 dollars of Yankee gold in his pocket, a saber, and a damned oath of allegiance that they made him put his mark on.

People were beginning to come toward him now.

Declaration of Independence—CDA Coeur d'Alene, Idaho
0600 Pacific Standard Time

The station manager had just turned the key in the lock when he was forced through the door. A large man with a pistol put the barrel on his nose and said, "Do what I say, when I say it or I will kill you now." The station manager could only nod affirmation. The large man pulled him to his feet and addressed him again. "You will play this cassette every 10 minutes until noon today. If you do not do exactly as I say, my men will kill your wife and son." The large man made a final comment before leaving the station manager to his assignment, "I want to thank you for the message that this stations projects about corrupt big government, out-of-control Liberals, and the invasion of this nation by non-white immigrants. You have helped to pave what will happen today."

The station manager dully looked at the cassette in his hand, his mouth gaping open, and his forehead knotted into concern for his wife and daughter. As he moved to the control room to perform his duty he questioned himself and his life's work, "I have been a big government protestor, a good voice for the conservative, and pulled for a return to the good old days. Could I have helped these maniacs?" The manager would soon bury his head in hands as he played the message.

"Be it known from this day forward that a New Nation exists separate from what was formerly northern Idaho. We declare freedom and independence from the United States of America." The clear voice of the Reverend, now General, spoke in clear and ringing words. "Be it known that this new nation will be called Columbia and be under the authority and guidance of the White American Nation." The General used a dramatic pause to let the information sink in. He continued, "Do not think that this is an unplanned prank. To insure that this new nation will remain unimpeded in its independence and autonomy, we have been forced to take drastic actions." Another dramatic pause was skillfully used by the General. "At this time a nuclear submarine is in the possession of the nation of Columbia. We have secured the nuclear weapons within this submarine and have the ability to detonate them."

"The following conditions must be maintained to keep the detonation from occurring: First, the borders of Columbia (formerly northern Idaho) to the 48th parallel will be secure from invasion by foot, ground vehicle, and aircraft. Second, no military movements or military build-up will occur within 100 miles of the nation of Columbia. Third, no action will be taken against our men in the nuclear submarine. Four, all non-white and unbelievers must leave Columbia by 10:00 a.m. today. If these conditions are not met completely, then one million people in Puget Sound will reach several thousand degrees Celsius in a mater of seconds."

The message ended and the station manager openly wept. His world had changed—not to his liking.

This same scene was duplicated in three other radio stations to varying degrees.

Security—Spokane, Washington
0715 Pacific Standard Time

There was little wind in Spokane for the morning radio message soon to be delivered. Each staircase door had been barricaded and Scout three brought up the video surveillance and armed the remote charges they had previously set.

Scout Two and One were completing the job on the rooftop door. While Scout One held the gas-charged canister of glycerin, Scout Two connected the fitting to the injection tube. One final check of the system and Scout One depressed the actuator that injected the pre-measured glycerin into the Iron oxide, aluminum, and potassium permanganate mixture. This design with the perforated inner tubing allowed for the Thermite reaction to occur evenly and with full effect. Thermite reactions had first been used by railroad workers in the early days to weld iron tracks when away from proper equipment. The Thermite reaction is very exothermic and melts steel easily.

Scout One said, "Fire in the hole." The only thing that could be seen at first was a slight bulging of the ceramic-coated tape and a bit of vapor under the duct tape. Then with an ever increasing crescendo, the reaction became fully involved. Acrid smoke drifted over the roof top and the seam between door and jam became red hot while miniature white bomblets erupted from the reaction and arched away from the door leaving a smoky trail. The reaction started to settle down and the red glow from molten metal was the only remainder of the violent reaction. The roof was secure.

Scout One spoke into his mike, "Check in." The order of the responses were well orchestrated, "Southwest—check. Northwest—check. Northeast—check." Scout One held the Southeast corner. Scout One turned on the small radio. The station was already selected. He waited for the declaration.

Scout One keyed the mike again, "Team, select first target." He heard a series of double clicks affirming his instructions." Scout One adjusted his telescopic sights on a state patrol car that had a motorist pulled-over on I-90. There job was to encourage chaos by targeting police and military. They waited.

The radio station interrupted the canned program and went directly to the taped message, "Be it known…" Scout One keyed the mike, "Engage."

The first round tore through the hood and incised a nice hole through the fuel injector housing and into cylinder number five of the state patrol cruiser. Smoke billowed out from the cruiser and the trooper moved to the front of the rig, saw the hole, and turned to look in the direction traced by the angle of entry. The second round the trooper's right foot between the second and third lace of his show. This was not a kill shot, but one intended to create fear and awe. The trooper's foot literally exploded. The 50-caliber round sliced through flesh and bone, hit the asphalt beneath the foot and sent gravel and steel back into the foot from below. The effect on the trooper was immediate. He was lifted from his standing position and launched onto the hood of his car. His food was a shredded piece of meat, bleeding profusely.

Scout One moved to his next target. He placed an incendiary round into the chamber and shook his head. He thought to himself, "I hate shooting these things. They don't fly straight and leave a mess in the barrel." His cross-hairs next rested on a fuel tanker delivering fuel into a station on Division Street, just a block from the freeway. The gun bucked. Scout One rested the weapon back into its place and looked through the sights. "Damn!" He cursed. The incendiary did not set off the fuel. The driver was next to the tank trying to plug the hole with a rag. He chambered a round, took aim, and put another hole over the rear set of wheels. The fuel flowed over the entire rear sets of wheels. Scout One then chambered another incendiary round and targeted the hub on the rear wheel. Seconds later he was rewarded with a fireball where the truck and driver once were.

Emergency vehicles were arriving at the state patrol cruiser. Scout One put a disabling round into each vehicle and a center-kill shot into every non-white who showed any part of a body. Interstate 90 was shut down.

Scout One thought to himself, "This is taking too long. We need more chaos and to expand the emergency quickly. Southwest, three kills—high school—copy?" Scout One spoke. A double click indicated the affirmative. Scout One looked through his scope into the upper floor of the high school across the freeway. He settled on a non-white teacher and squeezed the trigger. "One less to kill later," he thought. His next two kills were a non-white school security guard and another teacher. As he watched the pandemonium erupt from the school and the emergency vehicles begin to arrive, he heard the thump-thump rhythm of an approaching helicopter.

Scout One keyed his mike, "Turbine shot. Save the L.A.W.S. for later." The first airborne response was not police or military, it was a news copter. Northwest took careful aim at the turbine. A smile creased his face. He moved his cross hairs from the turbine to the rear rotor assembly. As the round struck the rear rotor assembly, the chopper quickly started to spin and yaw around its axis. The shooter smiled as the news copter began spinning slowly into the Spokane River. He thought to himself, "Good pilot; controlled crash."

The earphones crackled, "Motion in level one. They are coming through door one." Scout Four transmitted. Scout One responded, "How many?" "Looks like eight to ten." responded the scout on the northwest corner who had the surveillance and determent controls. No further communication was necessary. The contingency plan was well-rehearsed and on course.

Seven Spokane police officers and the building maintenance supervisor came through the door leading to the floor two floors below the roof. In the video, they moved in an effective tactical formation. The scout waited for the group to get within the kill zone and slowly depressed the first of ten push buttons. He felt a small thump through the roof; the video screen went completely white. Slowly, the screen began to clear and show the results.

The place was a mess. The ceiling tiles were broken and hanging; bodies lay crumpled near the center of the passage way. The bodies were still, except one who was slowly crawling toward the doorway. The police officer had a large piece of shrapnel in his leg and left a trail of blood down the carpeted hallway.

Concrete shards flew into Scout One's face.

THE ATTACK—CHAPTER 4

R.O.T.C.—Idaho-Washington State Line
0800 Pacific Daylight Time

Max Shelton didn't believe it. He could not fathom that his training sergeant was issuing him live ammunition and giving him rapid fire instructions. Until an hour before he was sleeping well in the air-conditioned dormitory at Eastern Washington University in Cheney. This was insanity.

The Sergeant started again, "All right boys! You are all qualified to operate your weapons, just listen to me or one of the other Sergeants. And for God sakes don't shoot unless we tell you when to shoot and who to shoot."

One of the other R.O.T.C. recruits voiced what all was thinking. "Sergeant, will we really have to shoot at someone? This has to be a mistake or a joke."

The Sergeant, an old crusty veteran of Desert Storm and the European campaigns lowered his head ever so slightly and exhaled slowly. "Boys," he began, "you need to catch what I say now and keep it close to your hearts. The people that we are going to most likely shoot at will be trying to shoot and kill you. This is not a joke or a drill. If you all listen carefully and follow my directions we will all live to expand our glory and forget that we filled our pants the first time a round buzzed by our ears. I know that none of you signed up for this when you went to college with R.O.T.C., but your country has called. Now boys! Saddle up!" The Sergeant grabbed his M-16 and grenade launcher, ammo bag, and rucksack and headed for the waiting duce-and-half.

As the Sergeant climbed in and sat down in the back of the venerable army transport truck, his mind took him to an earlier time. He was again back with those six fine young men that were his charge in Iraq. He was stationed with the Rangers at an advance staging area near a small village named Kali Aladam. His squad was to support the Rangers in cleaning out a nest of dug-in Iraqi Imperial Guard. The Rangers had just fragged and C-5ed one bunker when a trap door swung open between them and the Rangers. He had shot three Iraqi guards when his men started to take fire. He saw Smith and Martinson take rounds in face and Guadiaz and Washington take rounds in the legs.

When all was finished and done with, five of his six men were either wounded in action (WIA) or killed in action (KIA). The hell of it was that they had found no other enemy than the three. He was pretty sure that his men were taken out by friendly fire from the Ranger squad. His intimation of this fact and his refusal to modify his action report landed him R.O.T.C. duty in Spokane, Washington, for his last five years. The sound of voices and rattle of gear brought him back to the present.

As the column of young men, who less than a day ago had been sitting in college classrooms, grabbed their gear and headed for the trucks, the Sergeant made a silent prayer. "Lord, help me to keep these boys safe and to return to their families." A tear was quickly wiped from the Sergeants eye as he knew that the prayer would not be answered.

Max and the other troops in the caravan moved east on Interstate 90 toward the bridge at the Idaho State Line. The convoy skirted around the edge of North Spokane because of the sniper situation. Their mission was at the state line. As the trucks and other military vehicles arrived at the bridge, work was in progress to make a barrier at the bridge. While the bridge was a major passage way across the Spokane River, it was not the only way to Spokane.

The Sergeant saw the rough shod way that the barricade was being cted and walked quickly to the young Army captain and said,

"Sir Sergeant Bavairo with the Spokane R.O.T.C. group reporting." The captain looking frayed and harried began to ask for advice, but replied, "Very good Sergeant." The Sergeant being an old hand with young officers offered, "Sir, my group would be more than happy to construct the center barricade." The young captain looked meaningfully at the Sergeant and ordered him to "Carry on."

The barricade became a living barrier. This became a personal mission of the Sergeant and his young men. He first had four utility vehicles drained of their fuel and tanks filled with water. He then instructed that they be turned on their sides and cabled to the bridge piers.

Meanwhile, below the bridge, two reservists with the Idaho National Guard's 116th Brigade Combat Team placed shaped charged on the center span of both bridges.

All plans were in progress and the flanking sniper pits and light machine gun pits were in place when the bat phone buzzed in the make shift command post in the bunker-like weigh station one-quarter of a mile from the bridge. The inexperienced officer had chosen the weigh station as much for its operational view of the situation as for the creature comforts.

The Sergeant huffed with disapproval. He cursed under his breath as his group passed the command post and thought, "When will these young bucks learn that the best place for command and control is not in the only visible building for miles near a potential killing zone." His major would have demolished that structure so that artillery would not use it as a benchmark for directing their weapons."

The radio buzzed in the radio operator's ear and he reported to the young captain, "Sir, command reports that a large column is heading our way. They say to prepare for assault."

The captain yelled to those nearby, "Sergeants to your squads, prepare for action. Do not fire until the order comes from command."

As the Sergeant joined his men, he checked their positions and told them to prepare. "Lock and load; wait for my command to fire. You boys on the 60, remember, shoot low and let her buck up to the target. Flack jackets zipped all the way and cinch those helmet straps tight."

The sergeant remembered back to a time when he was the main 'rock-n-roll' star on the M-60 medium machine gun. He could still remember what his sergeant had told him and remember being surprised that the gun walked toward the sky anyway. He decided to amend his orders, "60 gunner, aim 20 feet in front of the vehicle. I want to disable them with a ricochet."

"That should do it," he thought.

There were a thousand other instructions he needed to give, but time was up. The first vehicles were small utility vehicles with eight occupants each. Two vehicles went to each side of the bridge and began frantic work to establish support positions. The sergeant saw what the enemy was going to do and yelled to the captain to request permission to dissuade the enemy. Minutes later the command came to remove the enemy positions.

The first sound was a single shot that sounded first like an M-80 during Fourth-of-July, then a metal tang. This was followed by three more in 15-second intervals. Max turned toward his sergeant and inquired, "Sarge, why don't we open up and take them out?"

The sergeant replied, "First you take away their method of retreat then you take *them* out. Son, what you heard was our sniper on that hill over there placing a nice neat round into the engine of each of those vehicles."

A whistle interrupted the quiet of the river followed by an explosion well to their rear. The Sergeant cursed, "the command bunker, damn." The captain came hurrying up to the Sergeant and gushed, "Sergeant, the command post doesn't answer my hail."

"Don't worry sir, the first round missed and the commander is now seeking friendlier ground," the Sergeant said convincingly. The Sergeant continued, "Sir we need to take out those mortars before they choose to use them on us. I suggest you order the sniper to fire at will and we get our mortars ranging." The captain was wise enough to realize who had the experience and in an unwavering voice said, "Do it, Sergeant."

The Sergeant picked up the bat phone and gave rapid fire instructions, "Pit one, three rounds in preset placement Charlie. Pit two, three rounds in preset placement Foxtrot. Commence!" Within twenty seconds the huffing of outgoing mortar rounds was heard. Three seconds later the sounds of explosions rented the air.

The silence that ensued after the explosions seemed wrong to Max. Things exploded, but the sound should be present afterwards. Max began to muse to himself, "What had his science teacher in high school said about the Doppler Effect? If the pitch... "Give me that weapon, son," the Sergeant was back. After Max handed him his M-16, he watched in awe as the Sergeant stood near the rear of the upturned vehicle and carefully took aim. Max peeked over the top of the side of the vehicle in time to see one man fall next to the road. Two more shots, two more fallen enemies. The Sergeant handed Max his weapon and barked, "Where is your second clip? Get some tape and tape it to this clip upside down." It took just 30-seconds of severe shakes to eternalize that his weapon had killed three human beings.

Max was broken from his thoughtfulness by the Sergeant talking on the bat phone. "Zulu, place a single round into each visible body to insure that they stay down." As Max watched, he heard the same M-80 bang followed now by a dull thud. He could only watch the first round strike and lift the prone body off the ground. His mouth began to water and the taste of gunmetal was dizzying as he stepped three paces away from the vehicle and spilled the contents of his stomach on the ground.

The young captain came quickly to the Sergeant's side. "Sergeant, what else do we need to do to prepare?"

"Captain, we need to set up a field of fire with these young scrubs. It will take about two hours to set everyone into the correct positions."

The captain pondered the time and said with a shaky voice, "Sergeant I need your help. The men look to you every time I give an order. I want you to take command of the squads and work with the other Sergeant."

The Sergeant nodded to the young captain and let him off the hook, "Captain, have a staff meeting at least twice a day with all sergeants. Also, sir, don't doubt your judgment. Give your sergeants the 'big picture' orders and trust them to carry out the fine points."

The captain regained his composure and thanked the Sergeant. He began to breathe with regularity again.

For the next three hours the R.O.T.C. scrubs were placed in very specific positions that limited their field of vision. The Sergeant had seen this used effectively in Kuwait by a Reckon squad in an oil field. The squad had placed themselves inside pipes that gave them protection and limited their vision range. This effectively gave a small force a lethal firepower and made an efficient killing zone.

The yellow glow of the Eastern Washington sunshine gave Max Shelton a warm, safe feeling. The feeling would not last. He could see his sergeant moving up the line toward him with additional clips for his M-16. When the Sergeant came to his position he looked intently into his eyes and squinted just a little. "Son," the Sergeant began, "keep off auto. Use the single shot setting and choose your targets."

Max interrupted the Sergeant, "Sir, when will we get to go home? When does the regular Army get here?"

The Sergeant straightened himself and put on his war face. The Sergeant barked, "Soldier, I work for a living—don't call me sir. Second, and most important, they don't tell you when you will be relieved. Just be ready." The Sergeant turned to leave, but stopped when Max lowered his head. The Sergeant softened and clasped Max's shoulder, "Son, just do what I say when I say it and we will all go home. I don't know when we will get relief, but I will keep you men advised." The Sergeant released the young man's shoulder and became the gruff old warrior again, "and soldier, prep that weapon."

As the Sergeant walked away, he shared some of the feelings of the young soldier. When would we get word from command he thought? When will we get a real fighting force? Just as he started to feel the cold creep into his spine, he heard the distance rumble. The Sergeant ran to the bat phone and clicked the transmit button and said, "Zulu, what do we have?" The Sergeant waited for what he thought was forever, but finally the static-rife voice came back, "Sarge, we got busses with a whole bunch of riders about two clicks out headed our way fast."

"Zulu, state force size."

"Command, thirty heavy vehicles and some light utility vehicles." The Sergeant wondered where the heavy track vehicles were. Don't complain for small favors he chastised himself.

The Sergeant called down the line, "lock and load." He turned his binoculars to the road on the other side of the bridge and scanned down the asphalt. He saw the yellow of the busses, but something was wrong, the buses looked wrecked. The buses were blurry in the optics and had multiple colors smeared across the yellow. What the devil was wrong with this picture?

The Sergeant lowered the binoculars and looked up and down the line. When he replaced the binoculars to his eyes, what he saw made his blood stop flowing and his breathe freeze in his lungs. The image brought to him was one from a nightmare of titanic proportions. He looked hard at the range finder knob of the binoculars and made a decision. The bat phone buzzed. He picked up the phone and answered the question asked by the captain, "Yes sir. No choice. Yes, sir." The Sergeant was glad that a small rise preceded the bridge from the east side. At least his men would not have to see the spectacle too soon.

Max now clearly heard the sound of vehicles on the highway in front of his position. The loud bark of the Sergeant telling his men to lock and load temporarily occupied his focus, but when he looked back in the direction of the sound he began to blink quickly. This same blinking happened to Max when he faced a difficult physics concept or calculus problem. This experience was not going to end in anything as simple as a solution to a problem.

All of the men on the line gave a collective gasp as they saw the unbelievable.

The Sergeant was the only one to speak, "Good God in heaven, it can't be."

Max beheld a nightmare scene closing on his location. The apparition was a school bus with guns bristling from the windows, but that did not elicit fear. What all focused upon were the people chained and roped to the outside of the buses.

Someone had welded small plates around the bottom of the bus and fitted the plates with human shields. The human shield was comprised of all sizes and types of humans. Some of the human shields were screaming; others' heads lolled like rag dolls with the rhythm of the bus. This war crime was sure indication that these freedom fighters had taken the path with no reconciliation, no quarter, and no mercy. This was a matter of survival.

The Sergeant came out of his haze of disbelief. A tear slowly found the least resistive track down his cheek. The words formed in his mouth and he barked out the order.

Flight Airborne—Mountain Home, Idaho
0330 Pacific Daylight Time

The otherwise peaceful night was rent with explosions and shouts. The young security guard was in the first stages of shock. She had been transferred to Mountain Home just last week after receiving her advanced security training at Lackland Air Force base. She was now puzzled at what had occurred. She could feel the blood oozing from the wound in her shoulder, but she could not feel her shoulder. What was wrong with that picture?

"Control the bleeding" a voice inside her head was saying. She slowly probed the area where her shoulder should have been but remained unfeeling and probed a small warm hole with her finger. She listened to the voice and plunged her index finger into the hole and moaned. As she rolled over, she saw a curious site. The tarmac appeared to be burning—NO, those were the aircraft she was assigned to guard. She could still see the muzzle flashes near the control tower. "Good," she thought, "we're still in this fight."

It was then that she first heard, and then saw, the two F-111B aircraft leap into the night sky. She had failed in her assignment. How was she going to explain this to her dad—she had lost two planes on her watch? She watched as another explosion rocked the airfield. This time the tower disappeared. The young security guard slipped into unconsciousness with a burning question in her mind, "Who were these bastards who invaded my world?"

"Alpha this is Bravo, fully loaded and ready to rock," came into the earpiece of the helmet. Alpha's pilot listened to his Bombardier respond to the call, "Bravo, go weapons hot, engage." The Bravo bombardier acknowledged that command.

The Alpha pilot fell into his own thoughts for a moment and tightened his grip on the joystick a bit. It had been seven years since he had last flown a 111. In his mind he thought, "Far too long." He still remembered the short discussion with his commanding officer. The Colonel had started by saying that he was the "best jet driver that he had ever known, but…" Alpha mused how one word had changed his life, "…but, your racial views are inconsistent with the modern Air Force. Your fitness report will indicate unsatisfactory and you will be required to participate in psychological evaluation." He remembered that the Colonel had screamed, "I have not dismissed you Major. Get your ass back in this office, NOW!" He had not stopped. He got in his truck and…

"…eight…zero. John, hey John!" his companion said through the helmet speakers and rapped his leg. "John, are you O.K.?" asked his bombardier. "Yeah, just off center for a minute."

"Take new heading one…eight…zero. The target is four…seven miles. Weapons hot," his bombardier announced.

John thought about how this could not be happening if this old bird wasn't such a survivor. They had found three pilots and two bombardiers in W.A.N. that flew the F-111. How ironic that these aircraft, fully loaded with arms were within fifty minutes flying time of all of their targets. "This mission was ordained by God," he thought.

John keyed his transmit button on his joystick, "Bravo, this is Alpha. Good hunting." Bravo responded in kind. By one of those quirks of nature, all four men had the same thought at the same instant, "We are going to make Idaho glow tonight."

The two aircraft separated. Alpha turned south and Bravo proceeded east. Both aircraft were taking their time. The wings were rotated to the full forward position and the Pratt and Whitney engines were gently singing at mid-throttle. Speed was not necessary for these sorties; precision was necessary. The beauty of the plan left the only two operational military jet aircraft at least two hours away at top speed. If the raiding party did their job as planned, the mission would get an additional hour to finish the task.

Alpha flight neared its target. "I have flight," announced the bombardier. Now John became the passenger for the bomb run. He watched as his bombardier flipped the 'ARM' switches to the 'ENABLE' setting on the outboard pods for the two incendiary bombs. He felt the bomb bay open and felt the drag slow the aircraft. He compensated by lifting the nose and pushing slightly forward on the power levers. The bombardier then enabled the four five-hundred pound bombs in the bomb bay.

Alpha's pilot mused how easy it was to get their comrades still in the Air Force to cut the orders and arm two F-111s with exactly the munitions needed to do the job. Everything was working just as planned.

The mercury vapor lights from the target were now in view. Not much of a target, but this night's mission would get a lot of people out of bed. John felt the release of the Napalm canisters, then a split second later the bombs released. He remembered flight training and was surprised when the instructor told him that Napalm canisters had a fairly good flight rate and flew to the target with the ship. "All yours," the bombardier said through his intercom. John immediately pushed the power levers to full afterburner and pulling back on the stick. This maneuver caused the wings to sweep back to a ballistic setting and effectively made the solid old F-111 a flying engine.

John rolled the aircraft into a shallow arc so that both men could see out their bubble-like cockpit at the impending explosion. John moved the selector on his helmet to slide his darkened visor from its sheath in his helmet. He needed to worry about night vision for at least for another hour or so. He had seen the sight of a strike on a target many times, but the first explosion always took him by surprise.

When the five hundred pound bombs hit the acetone, benzene, and other assorted solvents were thrown into the air as a cloud. When the napalm hit and ignited the entire pit was involved. The fifteen thousand stacked drums were ruptured, on-fire, and mixing with one another. The cloud of smoke and noxious vapors that rose from the fire began to slowly drift northeast toward Interstate 84, the small town of Bruno and the farming community of Glenns Ferry. Chemical warfare had reached the heartland of America. The ironic part of this fact was that it didn't arrive by a deal made with an unfriendly nation or from one of the military installations. This chemical warfare agent had come into being because of poor housekeeping and pork-barrel politics.

"Nailed it," cheered his bombardier.

The explosions continued with a crescendo with each napalm explosion. He could see drums flying into the early morning sky and felt a chill to think of what he had just release into the air. Their target was perfect to strike terror. Ecostore was nothing more than a pit filled with rusting drums of hazardous chemicals. The hope of the leadership was that enough of the drums contained flammable materials to feed the flames for days and spread the caustic and deadly smoke to Boise and beyond.

The bombardier interrupted the celebration and said, "secondary targets dialed in, take new heading zero-eight-five."

John responded, "Roger, new heading zero-eight-five, descending to 400 feet and slowing to loitering speed."

John continued to instruct, "Continue E.C.M. and E.S.M. Lets make sure no one else is out there."

The bombardier acknowledged his instructions and adjusted his scope to read I.F.F. and aircraft radar signatures. Just as he adjusted his scope, he got a solitary blip at the extreme range of his equipment for just a moment.

"Anything?" John asked.

The bombardier responded, "No, just warm up clutter. We're clear."

Meanwhile another pilot of aircraft that was of the same vintage as the F-111 was making his change from an observer to a hunter. The F-4 Phantom would have to live up to its name if Captain Cummings was going to have a chance of making a difference. Cummings had been absently tracking the jet since it took off from Mountain Home. His 'wild weasel' training mission was designed for him to use search radar to simulate S.A.M. radar sites.

He was surprised when the aircraft bombed the toxic waste site. His training kicked into gear and he went ship silent and descended to 300 feet. He rotated through the frequencies to find if Mountain Home or Boise were transmitting. He tried Guard Frequency. No joy! Things were radio silent. He could not transmit without fear of being detected, so he chose the rational path. He would watch this guy.

As his ancient, unarmed Phantom eased toward the earth he thought, "It doesn't look like I will make the eight o'clock tee off with the guys from pediatrics. Oh well."

Buck—Bangor Submarine Base, Washington
0500 Pacific Standard Time

Buck was not happy. No, he wasn't happy one damn bit. And when Buck wasn't happy, he did two things very well. He chewed cigars on the average of one per hour. The other was he made a living hell for those who got in his way. A submarine with terrorists on board, nuclear missiles, and he had just broken up with his fourth wife. "This is gonna be a doozy," Buck mused to himself.

As Buck got out of the Humvee at the dock, he saw three things. No one was in charge. Everyone was scared. A ballistic submarine was one big mother. He had sailed and operated with the boomers smaller cousin, the attack sub, as S.E.A.L. team leader. But, whew, this was a big piece of hole in the ocean.

A khaki-clad young man came running up to Buck just as he spit an inch of his stogie out on the ground. The lieutenant gave a sharp salute and said, "Sir, if you are Lieutenant Commander Pluncket, we need you immediately."

Buck returned the salute, gave the young man a glance, and growled, "Why?"

"Sir, the terrorists want to talk to someone in charge and say that they will execute the hostages," replied the lieutenant.

Buck said, "In that case I haven't arrived." The lieutenant started to say something, but thought better when Buck gave him the no-nonsense—I'm a S.E.A.L. look. Buck continued, "Lieutenant I want the senior-most chief of the boat, the engineering officer, and a missile technician. Now! I also want twenty welders here within five minutes." The young officer stood for only a moment, but then moved and started to bark out orders.

Buck started to think about his career, "Nine days and a wake up until twenty-five years in the 'NAV'." He would leave the Navy as a lieutenant commander because of an error made in the Persian Gulf. A senior diplomat wanted to give the Iraqis one last chance before the S.E.A.L.s blew up their oil rig in the Persian Gulf. His careless communication with the enemy caused the death of two of his men. He found the man, disabled him with a broken rib and separated shoulder. He was wiping what was left of one of his men's brain and blood in the diplomats face when he was tackled and restrained. The diplomat turned out to be the son of a senator and so his career was capped. He would do it all again.

"I have four welders standing by, sir," reported the lieutenant.

Another man accompanied the young officer. He was a forty something, burly man of six feet with Popeye type forearms. His crow insignia on his blue ball cap indicated that he was a master chief petty officer. His demeanor and bearing said that he was a fighter and he would not take crap from anyone.

The chief nodded at Buck and said, "Sir, those bastards got my boat." He bristled and scowled," I want her back, I am a jealous lover."

Buck took the man's hand a felt the grip of man accustomed to working on machinery. Buck released the Chief's hand and said, "Chief, we may have to lose the boat to save lives, capish?"

Before the older enlisted man could respond, the lieutenant interrupted and said to both men, "There are still twenty-five men aboard. The X.O. and…"

Buck cut the man with a glance and a simple statement, "Son, you do what I say, ask no questions, make no comments, and we will get along. Now, get what I wanted." Buck stopped the man as he went to do his bidding, "Lieutenant, I want to talk to the officer in charge of the S.E.A.L. team assigned to Bangor. I also want to talk to the C.O. of the air cavalry unit at Fort Lewis—move!"

The chief spoke again, "Sir…"

Buck interrupted him, "Chief, call me Buck when we are alone. We are the two who will fix this thing."

The chief smiled just a bit. The smile was seen by some as a grimace. His nose, broken thirteen times in different bar room brawls from Singapore to San Diego, made his face the road map of a deep water sailor.

The chief began, "Buck, we have twelve men who locked themselves in the engine room when the attack came. They control the rear one third of the boat."

"Chief, can this sub move with the men controlling that section?" asked Buck.

The chief smiled and responded, "No, sir." The chief continued, "I know the boys back there. They are now dog-earing the hatches and welding the dogs. The reactor is cold and the master interrupt switches for the batteries are in their section."

Buck spoke to the chief in a hushed volume, "Chief, I plan to have welders seal the missile doors to prevent launch."

The chief informed Buck, "Sir, they can't launch the missiles without the code and they can't arm the missiles without the code."

"Chief, one reason that I am here is that I am the guy that came up with the jury-rig solution for launching a missile and the C5 packet for starting the chain reaction." Buck shared.

The chief now looked scared. He had heard of the warning from ComSubPac about proximal use of C5 to start the reaction. "Holy, Mother of God," the chief prayed.

Buck addressed the shaken chief, "Get the welders started and cut all the power and communications with the sub."

Just as the Chief turned to leave a sound like a hot tub gone bad erupted from the front of the sub. The sound of large bubbles coming to surface was followed by men running toward the front of the sub.

Buck ran to the dock side and saw bubbles surfacing twenty meters in front of the sub and a body floating face down slowly leaking a crimson stain from several different places. Men quickly used a hook to lift the corpse to the dock.

The chief identified the man, "The X.O. They fired him through one of the forward torpedo tubes. That means that they have the missile room too."

Buck swung into action, "Get the men out of the engine room and get a raiding party into that section. Weld the missile hatches shut. Get me tha…" His ordering was interrupted by a small flash. He looked toward the conning tower of the sub. They were using the damn periscope to watch what was going on.

"Chief, secure that periscope," ordered Buck.

The lieutenant ran to Buck's side, "Sir, the terrorists say they have remotely wired the nukes to detonate. They want to talk to you."

Buck glared at the periscope now covered with a tarp and being chained to the side of the tower. He thought, now what?

As if someone had been listening to his inner voices a man in blue dungarees came running to him from the direction of the submarine's stern. The man in dungarees had bloodied knuckles and torn clothes. He walked purposefully up to Buck and began to speak.

"Are you in charge?" the newcomer stated. The lieutenant began to reprimand the newcomer for his lack of protocol, but Buck gave the JG a quick look as if to say, "Remember, what I said."

Buck said, "Yeah, this is my nightmare." He then asked a question of his own, "Who are you?"

The man said, "Missile Technician Third Class Seismore, sir."

Buck took stock of the young man. He was short of 5'8" tall, scrappy looking, and no nonsense. He appeared to be in his early twenties. What most spoke of the young man were his eyes. Those were the same eyes he saw in his fellow S.E.A.L.S. and looking back at him in the mirror each morning. This was a man with the heart of the warrior.

In reality the Missile Technician was a young man from Peshastin, Washington, who worked on his family fruit orchard until he graduated high school and joined the Navy. He used some of the football and wrestling training from high school earlier today.

"Sir, I was in the missile room when we were boarded," said the young man.

Buck was fully alert, "How many in the raiding party?"

The young man took several seconds to mentally count and then answered, "At least twenty. I'd say fifteen in the missile room and another five or six in the control room."

The young petty officer remembered when the attack began and how he thought that First Class Robbins had been kidding when he pulled the pistol and told the rest of the missile crew to stand against the bulkhead. He remembered that he first thought that this was just another silly drill. When Robbins had shot the new guy in the back of the head he had gasped, but then his instinct and rage took over. He tackled Robbins and drove him into the deck. He continued to pound the traitor until the other members of his crew pulled him off. His hands hurt, but the other man's face was a mass of blood and his jaw wasn't right.

He remembered that the hatch to the control room started to open and the muzzle of a gun pushed through. His section leader ordered the missile crew out of the missile compartment into the battery room and engine spaces. They quickly dogged and jammed the hatch.

The Petty Officer spoke again to Buck, "Sir, at least two of the crew was in on this."

Buck looked perplexed and saddened. How could any man betray his country and his shipmates? Those boys would have a special place in the special Hell that Buck designed.

"How many of the crew?" Buck asked.

The young man responded immediately, "Two for sure." He reported the important parts of the attack that were important, "The First Class in the missile room that won't chew for a while and a seaman from the galley who tried to shoot it out with one of the 'gyrines' in the engine spaces."

Buck nodded in affirmation and addressed the young man, "Stay right on my hip. You now are my expert on those damn missiles."

The young man just nodded and adopted his war face. The lieutenant again addressed Buck, "Sir the terrorists say they will detonate the missiles unless you meet their demands immediately."

Buck turned to the young man, "Can they have jury-rigged those things this fast?"

"No way!" the young man said while shaking his head. "I'm the best and it would take me at least one hour to redirect the circuitry, remove the arming/failsafe guards, and place the explosive charges to detonate," the young man finished.

A load sound again came from the front of the submarine. Buck turned to see what his next step would be.

CULMINATION—CHAPTER 5

Cleansing—Athol, Idaho
1540 Pacific Standard Time

The members of W.A.N. had many meetings considering how to treat the non-whites and the sympathizers after the takeover. The leadership learned from history that when a perceived atrocity existed, people were more likely to be brainwashed by a corrupt government. Many of the planning meetings went by with plans that detailed shipping by rail and busing out of Columbia. Many advocated a much simpler solution, but clearer heads prevailed.

In those days the Reverend spoke of bringing the chosen whites who had strayed back to his flock. He provided his faithful with a clear lesson of separating the sheep from the goats and about the lost sheep. He preached that they needed a place where the lost sheep could hear the truth and be brought back into the fold.

One Lieutenant suggested using an auditorium, but that idea was rejected because of the difficulty in defending the site from outside assault and inside revolt. This item remained under old business in Trident planning meetings for many months. The needed requirements were many, however, the most important were ease of command and control, all basic human needs self-contained, and small contingent of troops required to secure and operate the site.

Then, came the day of revelation; the solution not more than fifty miles from the compound. The revelation came through the United States mail in the form of a coupon.

The amusement park lay situated an hour north of Coeur d'Alene and resided on a small rise that overlooked the surrounding country.

The entire facility was fenced and had a state-of-the-art security system. The approach from the northwest had a three hundred meter cleared area. Whoever designed this facility provided the W.A.N. faithful with a killing field second to none. Power, water, and waste were self-contained. The generator could power the 'camp' for nearly a year with conservation. Water was from a well and the waste disposal system was excellent. Even the solid waste was fed through a small incinerator that provided steam for electrical generation or heat. Camp Columbia was a perfect place for re-education and changing thinking to the correct frame.

From a tactical point of view, the camp only required three shifts of five marksmen to insure order. Along with ten re-education troops inside the perimeter to work in shifts changing lives Trident could easily operate this facility with less than thirty faithful.

The amusement park became Camp Columbia one-hour after the radio announcements began declaring the insanity that would follow. The guards at the gate had put up no defense. In fact three of their numbers joined the group immediately. One guard, however, was not the right color and made the mistake of reaching for his pistol. He was one of the first casualties of Trident. Camp Columbia would grow to 1300 people within the first day of operation. Many of those numbers would never leave the gates. Many who left the gates wished that they had not.

Planning Pays—Spokane, Washington
0925 Pacific Standard Time

The concrete stung like hell. Scout One wheeled around and saw a flash from a scope on the building to the west. He immediately took cover behind the potted tree. Another ricochet careened off the concrete wall, no damage. "Northwest stand by charge one target sierra." The scout spoke into his radio. He saw his colleague move a guarded cover away from a toggle switch and look his way. He spoke a single word to cause so much damage, "Activate." Before he had finished the word completely the top of the building became shrouded in dust and smoke.

Scout One had no idea what the other scout had rigged on that particular rooftop, but it appeared to be effective. Their number had been to Spokane on five different occasions and prepared defenses for this very reason.

After the dust settled and the smoke blew away with the prevailing western wind, the damage was clearly visible. The retaining wall on the roof of the building was literally peeled away from the roof. Much of the debris fell to the street. Few people were hit by falling masonry because few were on the streets once the shots were heard. The three strings on heavy duty primer chord did the trick. The scout that rigged that rooftop wanted to take away all chance of cover and to send a clear message. The level of destruction was impressive even to him.

The scouts continued to select targets and cause chaos.

After another twenty minutes with the big gun, Scout One keyed his mike, "Switch to mortar. Nine rounds and remember walk the rounds ten degrees each time." There followed a small silence interrupted by three sets of affirmative by clicking the mike twice. It took only eight minutes for each man to set the mortar and prepare the rockets.

The scouts kept a close eye for activity from other rooftops, but for the moment all was quiet. The injured police officer had dragged himself down one flight of stairs and was quickly rushed to medical services. The video feed provided a vision of a hallway with bodies and little else. Each scout knew that they were in a period of time called the 'Golden Moment'. This was the period of time between fifteen minutes and one hour when all of the experts were called and staging was mounted. The mortar attack should slow down the response. Scout One reflected, "They lasted far longer than I thought they would. Any time longer was a gift."

The mortars were set at 45 degrees from the vertical to get the greatest range from this elevated position. This would provide an attack of 36 separate bombings in all parts of the city. It would appear as if Spokane were under general attack. It would create chaos. Scout One looked at his watch and keyed his mike, "Fire!"

One Man—Coeur d'Alene, Idaho
0700 Pacific Standard Time

John Cloud was mad. He openly cursed. He had just heard the declaration of independence for the nation of Columbia. All non-whites must leave? What kind of joke was this? He heard the same message repeated over and over. They had the radio stations. That made John furious. John was not a man who was used to waiting for things to happen. He made them happen.

John had been teased in Navy boot camp about his looks, his heritage and his name. His mother and father had chosen to drop him off at the Tribal Headquarters when he was only one week old. The note attached to the box that contained him, a bottle, and several diapers sat on the steps when the secretary arrived on Thursday morning. The note said that John's dad was from the Colville and his mom was Yakama. The couple wanted to travel and did not want to live on the reservation, but wanted their child to grow up with his people. The informed the reader that his name was John, but that he should take the name of the family who adopted him.

Thankfully, the secretary who found the bundle brought him home and her husband agreed. John grew up in a loving home in Nespelum, Washington, where he learned to hunt, fish, and understand honor. After boot camp, John made the grade to become a S.E.A.L. He had spent twenty years in the Navy and then came back home to teach on the reservation. He was a member of the Sheriff Tactical Command and maintained a reserve status with the Navy.

John parked his pickup six blocks from the radio station and quietly donned his tactical gear. One of the jobs he had trained for and was good at was medium range sniper. This meant that he was an extremely good shot and could shoot and move with a standard weapon.

It took John full 20-minutes to make his way to the station. He had evaded the roof top guard. He moved with great stealth into the building adjacent to the broadcast building. It took him another ten minutes to get his target into the right place where he would not make noise when he fell. His weapon was not silenced, but it only made a coughing sound when fired. His target was sitting on a maintenance trunk when John made a slight whistle. His adversary looked right at him, opened his mouth and John shot his square in the mouth. The man slumped backward without struggle or movement. The bullet had traveled through his mouth, slammed through his cervical vertebrae that threw a shower of bone throughout his spinal cord, carotid artery and esophagus. John thought to himself, "Target One down."

John moved into the radio broadcast building very slowly. He saw the trip wire with the grenade by the front entrance and knew that he was dealing with amateurs. He heard a urinal flush down the hallway. This guy was very careless. When the guard opened the door he had no time to react when the barrel of a rifle was jammed into his mouth. He dropped his own weapon and would have relieved himself again if he had any urine left in his bladder. John motioned the man out of the restroom and told him to quietly back down the hallway toward the office. He asked the man how many others were in the building, but the man was far too frightened to respond.

John rounded the corner into the office and a sudden commotion erupted from the right. His captive was pulled from his grasp and ended against the far wall with a balding, round-bellied man on top of him beating him with fists and elbows. He let the man continue until the invader was unconscious, and then said, "Enough! I want this one alive."

Over the next five hours, John Cloud liberated all of the radio stations in Coeur d'Alene. He killed when he had to and took prisoners when he could. One man could make the difference.

Stockpile—INEL Attack—Arco, Idaho
0500 Pacific Standard Time (Bravo)

Bravo Flight was cruising at 400 feet using the ground following navigation system. There was probably no reason to evade in this way, but training was training. His F-111 was coasting without much effort and he had time to use the interphone to review the attack plan with his bombardier. "Stan, pull up the aerial photo from the site and place it on screen three," the pilot spoke into his helmet mike. In an instant screen three flickered from the navigation information to the full color aerial photograph of the Idaho National Engineering Laboratory. Stan keyed his mike and started his review, "Look at the northeast quadrant of the map and find the old domed reactor building." He continued, "The reactor is not active, but what we want sits outside the main door on pallets and inside the maintenance area. The low and medium radioactive waste is stored in stainless steel drums that are welded shut."

In fact, some of the drums were regular oil drums from the 1950s. The United States could not get their long-term radioactive storage facility approved; therefore, there sat stacks of radioactive waste in steel drums awaiting purposeful disturbance in the Idaho desert. This was a recipe for disaster.

The plan is to create a radioactive cloud from the burning waste. Bravo Flight spoke again to the man who sat next to him in the cockpit, "Is the plan intact?"

The plan was to make the first approach with one of the standard 500 pound Rockeye bombs that would rip the containers open and spread the contents of the drums in a nice open mass. The approach would maximize the old reactor building as a backstop. The bomb would hit the drums explode at their leading edge of the stack. The explosion would throw the drums and their contents toward the concrete wall of the reactor where they would bounce off and lay exposed to the air in a pile for the first time in decades.

The next run would be the fire starter. He would place his incendiary munitions so that the contents would spray over the opened contents of the drums and the wall of the reactor. The final run would be to fire one of his sidewinder missiles toward the heat source. He hoped to skid the missile across the pavement under the pile of burning waste and aerate it even more.

If Bravo Fight could make all of the correct runs and place munitions on target, then a roiling radioactive fire would create a deadly cloud that only God and the winds could know the full effect.

Stan answered, "All munitions on-board checked and ready." Stan thought of the upcoming strike and smiled. This was the kind of thing that he lived for. Stan keyed his mike, "Bravo leader we are 10 miles from target. The approach line is perfect. I have the aircraft."

Bravo Leader thought to himself that in less than five minutes he would help strike a blow against the corrupt American Government that pushed him away for the likes of the non-whites. What did Reverend Stewardt say? "All of the ills can be washed away in a great Godly wave that will begin with our struggle and gather tributary support until the flood is unstoppable and overwhelming to all who stand against us." The pilot of Bravo Flight sat back in his ejection seat a bit and thought, "No one can stop us now."

The sun was beginning to bring real illumination to the high desert of Idaho. Chuck Martin sat on a small outcropping of rock on a slope of one of the small hills near the Idaho National Engineering Lab. He was off-duty and out of contact. His high pressure job as security chief for INEL left him little down time and less time for him to get away into the wild. He was hunting elk. He had parked his old pickup five miles away and had hiked since shortly after midnight to get to this promontory at this time of the morning. He leaned his 7mm Magnum against the rock ledge and stretched. He knew that today he was going to bag a kill; he felt it in his bones.

As he starched he saw the shadow approach. An aircraft was moving toward his position at low altitude. This was wrong. The aircraft was already in violation of a no fly zone, he thought. The direction that he was flying would take him directly over the laboratory. "What was that pilot thinking?" he asked himself. As he watched the aircraft continued its course and nearly overflew his position. Chuck cursed, grabbed his weapon and scampered to the top of the hill to view INEL not more than six miles away. The aircraft was flying toward the place he was hired to protect.

The Bravo Flight bombardier marked his target with the cursor and the F-111 made small corrections in its flight path. Stan jolted in his seat when the bomb bay doors opened with a whine followed by a clunk. The power levers were pushed slightly forward to compensate for the drag of the opening in the airframe. While the bomb run was in progress the pilot did little except help manage the flight of the aircraft. This gave him a wonderful opportunity to see the early morning beauty of southern Idaho and make out some of the detail of the approaching target. He could now see the stacks of drums piled against the reactor wall.

The bombardier awaited the tone from the targeting computer and depressed the 'pickle' switch so quickly that it seemed like he chose the time rather than the computer.

Casper—The Dams-Snake River Dam near Bliss, Idaho
0500 Pacific Standard Time

Captain Cummings was known by the call sign that he received when he was a nugget flying off the Enterprise. He was unceremoniously dubbed Casper after the friendly ghost. His commander at the time had said he was the best at stealth intercept, but didn't pull the trigger fast enough. He liked the ghost part, but didn't appreciate the friendly part.

Tonight the full bird Captain in the Navy Reserve did not have to worry about pulling the trigger—he was unarmed. He would continue to monitor and be able to coordinate an attack on this bogie if he made another aggressive move. For now he would stay low and slow, light out, and radiation silent and watch this guy.

Alpha leader took control of the venerable F-111 again and turner ten degrees south of east. He keyed his mike, "25 minutes to secondary target." For just a moment the two men looked at one another and both grinned at the same time. Each knew that their next target was the dream of pilots and little boys since planes carried bombs.

The Alpha flight continued east at a leisurely rate; they knew that they were safe and that all interceptors were full of holes sitting on the tarmac at Mountain Home Air Force Base. By this time the A-Team from the White American Nation would be moving through the sagebrush and evading. "God willing" he thought "they would make it to fight another day."

Casper followed at a safe-from-detection range. His right hand itched for just one sidewinder to pickle-off his wing, but he knew that would not happen tonight. He was the eyes and ears tonight. Casper thought of his many sorties over the Gulf in both wars. During the first Gulf War, he was a young man; barely a Lieutenant. During the second Gulf War, he led a Naval Reserve squadron of F-4 Phantoms on S.A.M. (surface to air) suppression missions. He and all of his pilots were younger than the planes they flew, but he had no desire to fly any other bird. The Phantom was loud, powerful, and rugged. In addition to these features, it could carry an enormous payload of weapons. His bird was one that had an upgraded avionics package that included Fast Scan Radar (F.S.R.), advanced Electronic Counter Measures (E.C.M.), and something that was still fairly confidential—a thermal detector with a range of twenty miles.

The F.S.R. provided a quick peek at an enemy. The one-trillionth of a second scan rate was juiced-up with a detector that was two orders of magnitude more sensitive than conventional radars. The trainers said it was like opening a door a fraction of an inch on a clear night ten miles away. The F.S.R. scan was also random. This gave the operator on the other end something that could easily be dismissed as clutter and quickly decrease the gain to compensate for noise in the system.

The Electronic Counter Measures would absorb radar radiation from another source and send a scattering signal in return. It would not completely eliminate the radar signature of the F-4, but it would make it very small and fleeting. The upgrade in his ship was the same installed in the A-6 Specter aircraft that preceded the main attack from a Carrier Air Group. He hoped that the guys at Raython were correct about the electronics.

His favorite new toy was the thermal detector. He could identify a small flame one mile away or the exhaust from a jet at ten miles. He was now employing this new technology to track the F-111. He could stay at the other pilot's six and appear to be an echo from the tail and elevators.

The pilot from Alpha flight looked below and saw that the featureless desert was dissolving to canyons and coulees. One minute later he saw that the aircraft was following a large river that he knew to be he Snake. He had fished the Snake River up high in Idaho where it was pure and fast. In this reach of the river only muddy side channels and the occasional rapid marked the wide muddy river. He looked out his left window and saw the town of Glenns Ferry pass beneath him. He knew this little town from his childhood.

His father had brought him to the celebration held each year to commemorate the Oregon Trail crossing the Snake River. He also remembered how the horses pulling the wagon had fallen into the deep part of the river and struggled until one horse had drowned and the other had finally found its footing and found the other bank. He had quailed at the site and began to whimper. His father had cuffed him and told him to stop acting like a girl.

The bombardier broke the silence, "Alpha lead, I have target number two on the scope and in the zone. Prepare to go flight to my controls." The pilot looked in the far distance and saw the blue of the lights shining from Bliss Dam. Alpha leader said, "you have control of the aircraft. Let's see if a dam is as impregnable to conventional bombing as often cited."

Casper saw the change in the radar signal and new that the F-111 was making another run. The ghost was about to make himself more visible. The Captain eased his nose up and pushed the power control ever so forward. He started to close the distance between bandit one and himself. He thought to himself, "I guess I will miss that tee time."

The wolf pursued his prey while the watchful shepherd watched the wolf. The air of Southern Idaho was quickly becoming a poisonous soup and the aircraft flew onward.

Engagement—Idaho-Washington State Line
0800 Pacific Daylight Time

"Sniper, take out the rear tires, NOW!" barked the Sergeant in the bat phone. He continued to give instructions to the rest of the troops, "Hold your fire until instructed. Take aim at any spot where people are not."

The sniper abandoned his cover and moved his body to rapid fire position. His spotter took three rounds out of the canvas and sheep skin magazine that he carried. He had spent hours creating this completely quiet and fast access cartridge magazine for the 50-caliber rounds of the sniper rifle.

The sniper took careful aim at the left rear tire of the bus. He aimed so that his round would take out two tires on that side of the bus. They had left him only a six inch gap between the human armor and the tire well. He squeezed off the round. As was the norm with this weapon, it took 10-seconds for all of the sense to return for a second shot. He had ejected the spent round, accepted the offered replacement from his spotter and slammed the bolt forward, flipped the bolt handle, and double-locked the bolt. He then centered his weapon again on the bus and looked through the scope. The outside tire was flat, but the inside tire had survived. He then saw that the tire was slick looking with a reddish tint. He followed the line of the tire for another shot and saw the woman's leg gushing blood. It appeared that the round had entered her right calf and blew a big hole in calf muscle. The woman lay slack against her bonds, her hair blowing around her face.

The bat phone clicked, but he did not hear the words as he squeezed off the next round. The projectile traveling at one and one half the speed of sound entered the flattened tire, remained on course and hit the inside tire. After it was finished with the tire it ricocheted into the brake line. The air line separated and the air quickly evacuated from the lines as well as the air tank. As the air went out of the system the dynamiters closed the brake pads onto the wheel cylinder. All of the wheels stopped rotating at the same instance and bus came to a skidding controlled stop. The sniper's second shot had made up for the first shot.

The sniper started to rise and help the woman that his first round had injured. A strong hand of his spotter grasped his shoulder partly in a motion to stop his movement and partially from a sense of comradeship. The sniper sank back into his nest.

The spotter got on the bat phone and spoke to the Sergeant, "Bus disabled, one friendly injured, request to eliminate unfriendly targets of opportunity." What the young spotter had just asked for was permission for a hunting license. If granted, any unfriendly that made an aggressive move was fair game.

Before the message could be responded from the Sergeant, the second vehicle passed the first bus. This was an older model Bradley Fighting vehicle with the words 'Idaho National Guard' emblazoned across both sides. Following the Bradley were a deuce-and-a-half, another school bus, and a variety of civilian vehicles. They stopped just short of the bus and the men inside deployed to positions.

The Lieutenant quickly ran to the Sergeant's position and looked over the barrier as the first rounds began to ping of the protective metal. His eyes met the Sergeant and his lips began to move. The Sergeant spoke first, "Sir, it is time to release the hounds. Give permission to engage." The young Lieutenant might pay for this decision later, but he too saw the dead and dying shackled to the bus. He gave the order to his subordinate, "Sergeant, give the order—Fire at will! Targets of opportunity!"

The Sergeant wasted no time, "Sniper, weapons free—good hunting." The Sergeant continued, "Pit one, Pit two, target vehicle to the rear of the bus. Use low yield to target then pour it in." The Sergeant finished his orders and heard the first 50-caliber rip into the enemy line. He turned to his young R.O.T.C. riflemen, "Boys, do not rapid fire. This is an exercise of marksmanship not laying down lead." He continued, "Fire at any target of opportunity."

The Sergeant moved down the line to where Max Shelton and two other young men lay clustered in the prone firing position. "You three fire at any opening or muzzle flash on that Bradley. Keep them busy. Don't aim for the engine or other parts—just the openings." The Palestinians had taught the Israeli Army a costly lesson about the way that the Bradley had to open shooting slots to fire from the vehicle. Once a round entered the armored vehicle, it bounced and ricocheted around until finding human flesh.

Suddenly, one of the opposing forces ran to the side of the bus and began to shoot those still alive who acted as human armor. The Sergeant saw the man take four rounds at almost the same time. He was proud of his young riflemen. The concussions of mortar fire quickly made a terrible killing zone around the bus. As quickly as the mortars fell on their targets, the sound of incoming mortars was heard. The targets were clearly the two mortar pits. Now it was a matter of who was best and quickest.

The unfriendly mortars started to walk toward Pit one. In an engagement for existence, Pit one fired back. This exchange occurred for three rounds each. The final round from both mortar crews found home. Pit one was disabled—no response from the crew, but the unfriendly mortar crew was toast as well. He saw that the reserve mortar crew was moving toward Pit one to check for casualties and to reset the mortar position.

The Sergeant moved up and down the line to check on his men. He passed one young soldier who was bloody in the face and neck that was still taking aim and squeezing his trigger to no effect. The Sergeant called for a medic and gently moved the man to a sitting position behind the overturned rigs. He gently removed the damaged

M-16 from the young man's grasp. The weapon had sustained a direct hit in the magazine. The shrapnel from the destruction peppered the young man's face and neck, but nothing looked too bad. This young man would survive to fight yet today.

Soldier, you took a round to your weapon. You are O.K.; just some shrapnel wounds to impress the ladies. Look at me!" the Sergeant barked. The young man focused, his gaze first went blank, then his face became flushed and his jaw set in anger as he addressed the Sergeant, "Sarge, can I have another weapon—I'm ready to fight." The older man clasped the younger man's shoulder and gave him his own M-16 and told the soldier to let the medic treat his wounds.

The last vehicle in line suddenly erupted in flame and moved back six inches. Holy crap! The bad guys had a grenade launcher or R.P.G. (rocket-propelled grenade). The Sergeant peered through a hole in the overturned vehicle and saw a recoilless rifle mounted on Toyota pickup. The shooter was hidden from view behind the bus and had a living victim in direct line to the breech of the weapon. The Sergeant saw a puff from the muzzle and ducked his head.

Reports—White American Nation Compound (near Bunker, Idaho)
0500 Pacific Standard Time

General Jim Stewardt continued to pace the communication center in the compound. The control and exclusion zone had pushed-out another 10 miles around the compound. He was still wary and wanted more security. The General was fretting about the same things that all generals fretted-over on the eve of the attack. The 'what ifs…' were mounting and the electronic sounds of the radios, printers, and varied computer hardware seemed to pierce his mind and sound like a raging hurricane. He calmed himself by remembering what brought him to this place in his life.

As a child the General had grown up in and among the lesser races. He had watched as drugs, beatings, and gangs consumed those of lesser blood. His chosen vocation had not originally been to serve the Lord in the great cleansing, but as a pianist. At an early age his parents had provided him with the piano and the training to expand his near savant ability. Jim Stewardt, the pianist, ended one clammy October evening when his home and his life were forever violated. The newspapers reported that the destruction of his young life was a 'random act'. He remembered that the door had burst open in the middle of the William Tell Overture. The men who invaded his home wore masks, but he could see the color of their arms and hands. He watched as the beat his father senseless and savaged his mother. His thoughts were interrupted by the communications officer.

"Sir, Trident Two reports that they have control of the submarine and are beginning the process of making the weapons accessible," the communications officer reported. The wording was not lost on the General. The meaning of the message was clear. Trident Two would be able to manually detonate nuclear weapons within several hours. Trident Two was proceeding nicely.

The General returned to his thoughts. When the men had finished on his mother, they took turns choking her to near death and then allowing her to regain full consciousness before again bringing her to the brink of death. This continued for three cycles until one of the men became careless and choked too long. His father's chest stopped rising and falling at about the same time as the men began to kill his mother.

He remained on the floor while the men ransacked the house, collected valuables and spoiled his family's possessions. When the men were ready to leave, they turned their attention to him. The beat him and threw him into walls. He only remembered the first several blows and the first wall. He awoke days later in a hospital bed. His Aunt Mary sat next to his bed holding his hand. She was crying, her eyes were red and she held a Bible in her left hand. He knew that his parents were dead, that was no surprise.

What troubled him the most was the fact that little was being done to find the men who destroyed his world. The police detective who stopped by and took his statement said that it was going to be hard to find the perpetrators as the entire neighborhood was filled with suspects. The single event that changed the direction of Jim Stewardt's life was not the loss of his parents, the beating or the helplessness, it was the burly man wearing a cross and carrying a Bible that told him that God had sent him to find the men who did this to his family and bring justice to Earth. Reverend Morgan was a former pastor who could no longer turn his eyes away from evil, but attacked it with a vengeance. He was a tool of God and the young Jim knew his calling.

The bodies of three black men were found a week later on the front stoop of Jim's house. All dead and all marked with the sign of the Templar. He and Reverend Morgan worked to bring justice for twenty years after Jim had completed his education at the Seminary. His advisors told him that his radical and bigoted views were inconsistent with church doctrine and that he would not be called for a pastor's job in the near future. Jim had accepted that and went about the business of justice and creating his own flock.

The communication officer spoke again, "Sir, Trident Three is preparing to make their first run. All quiet and proceeding according to plan." The communication officer placed his fingers against his right earpiece and repeated the words that he was currently hearing, "Trident One High has begun their attack."

General Stewardt turned from his command and control team, clenched his fist and bowed his head. He spoke a simple phrase, "His will be done."

COUNTER—CHAPTER 6

Night Stalker—Pend d'Oreille River near Cusick, Washington
2330 Pacific Standard Time

Sam Becker and his team had crossed the Pend d'Oreille River by small boat several times that night already. His mission was simple, invade the enemy territory, establish a foothold, take prisoners, and eliminate non-whites. As he crossed the river again, he remembered the last crossing. His team had surprised the family of non-whites and took six prisoners, but sadly the father of the family put-up a fight and had to be dispatched. Sam thought, "The only sad thing was that this guy did not put up a better fight."

Sam Becker did not have an easy childhood. The men on his father's side of the family raised the boys in the family for a mission. Since their great-great grandfather, the Colonel, Becker boys were striking a blow for whites. His grandfather has laid the leather strap across Sam's legs until they bled and swelled to twice their size for taking part in a Ku Klux Klan rally.

With every blow his grandfather would recite the litany handed down from his father and from his father, "Beckers make a difference! Beckers don't join, but lead! Make every kill for riotousness and give quarter to no one! Two types of beings occupy this world: White People and Subhuman Non-whites!" Sam had learned the lesson well. He had killed many times. Sometimes it was for retribution and others for justice. Most of the killings appeared to be random in nature; and little evidence remained for the crime lab to find. Whenever he left evidence it clearly pointed to a non-white persuasion.

He would abduct a felonious non-white, take him to the site of the cleansing and leave his DNA evidence, fingerprints, and other identifying evidence. Afterwards he would return the abducted non-white to his home, stained with blood and the knife hidden in his house. He would watch the news for several days and laugh when the non-white perpetrator maintained his innocence even though the physical evidence was overwhelming. Sam was glad that this new foray into purity was more straight-forward.

Becker's Team was nearing the west shore and their target was in sight. They would grab prisoners or dispatch those who resisted. The whites were bound for re-education, while the non-whites for internment with little but shipment to their country of origin as any possibility. Sam wondered why the Reverend even allowed the choice. A bullet was a lot cheaper than a bus ticket, his old grand dad had always said. In Sam's case his specialty was stealth and a sharp blade. At the last place, he used one of his Gerber skinning knives to cut the man's carotid in a single rapid stroke. The knife was out of its scabbard, into the man's neck, and back into the scabbard in less time than most men use to take the safety off on the firearm. He liked to kill with the skinning knife because it slashed and sliced; it did not stab. The opponent died from hemorrhage and severe exsanguination. He liked to see his foe die and for his foe to know that he was dying.

The group had taken 75 prisoners in the last two nights of operation and had thirteen enemy killed in action. Terror was beginning to spread in this eastern-most border of Washington State. After the announcement this morning, the place was a bit more on guard, but it was still an easy mission to complete.

The boat barely touched the opposite shore when Sam's team leapt to action. The muffled outboard made little sound and the team made even less. Sam gave hand signals to his men to take flanking moves to the right and to the left and await his final signal to move in.

As he watched his men to the right flank move forward, he saw the muzzle flash from a rifle, followed by the blast from a shotgun. Both of these discharges came from the wrong direction and were not weapons that his men carried. Sam thought, "Damn, some cowboy saw my men." Sam reached to his interphone mike switch and clicked it three times. This was the signal for the team to move in and take out the target. The prisoner gathering was a bust; it was time to eliminate any hostiles.

Soon after clicking the microphone switch, a large explosion resounded from the position of the muzzle flashes. He stood and moved toward what was left of the sniper position. As he moved forward, one of his team leaders returned with the news that the target was empty. Just as the man finished with his report a shotgun blast ripped into his head and shoulders leaving little of the man and only gore of death remained. He moved quickly to intercept the shooter. As he did so he found himself on the ground with a heavy weight on his back.

He performed a suplex move that spun his assailant off and allowed him to get to a crouch. He had hardly stood and barely ducked the blow that came quick and sharp. He pulled his K-Bar fighting knife and thrust for a solar plexus blow, but was blocked. Sam thought, "Damn, this guy is good. His hand to hand is almost equal to mine." As the hand came in again he grabbed, wrenched, leaned his body and brought the K-Bar to his opponent's throat.

As he slid the blade for the death blow, he knew something was wrong. The feel of the blade was all wrong; it didn't feel like flesh and cartilage of the neck, but of bone and muscle. Somehow the other had moved his hand between the knife and the blade. As he paused in a state of wonder, his opponent countered his move, grasped the K-bar in a reverse wrist lock and was moving the knife to his throat. A moment before his death or his next move, a pistol shot rang out and his assailant lay still.

Sam was shaken. He had never been bested in a fight, and now he would never know if this man would have won. The other man from Sam's team helped Sam to his feet. Both men went over and shined their red-filtered flashlight on the worthy opponent. What both saw brought wonder to each man in different ways.

The opponent was clearly a woman. She must have been in her mid-twenties, 5 foot ten and muscled like a man. She was a fighter by choice looking at her broken nose. It was then that he saw the Marine Corps tattoo on the upper right arm. Sam's companion spoke first, "Holy Moley, she is an Amazon." Sam recovered and said, "She is the toughest man I have ever fought."

The two men moved back to the remainder of the squad. Two men were carrying two dead of their numbers. Sam addressed his team, "Did you confirm the other body? I saw two discharges too close together to be from one person."

One of his team answered, "We found a blood trail that went into a thicket of woods. We stopped and came back when you sounded the recall."

Sam hated loose ends and this was one hell of a loose end. The men moved quickly from the bank of the river into the boat and across the water silently. They had taken their first casualties. "Damn, that woman could fight," thought Sam. This incident had shaken his confidence, but his machismo and undaunted superiority quickly kicked-in. His next insurgency into hostile territory would be different. He would succeed. Tomorrow night they will enter completely as ghosts; he will bring only the best troops along on the next foray. He also would not take prisoners; this part of the mission will be the create terror and chaos part of the job.

Sam Becker sensed the impact of a high velocity round and then heard the report of the rifle.

Camp Columbia—Athol, Idaho
1905 Pacific Standard Time
The theme park had been renamed Camp Columbia. There were three sections of the camp clearly marked and separated with fence and armed guard. The Reverend-General Jim Stewardt had made it

clear that each person would be given three chances to convert to the tenets of the White American Nation and take allegiance to this group. The areas were divided into these three sections. New arrivals would be placed in Section One where they would receive orientation and re-education. If the person was a true white in their thinking and their person, they would move to Section Two. This would satisfy the first call.

In Section Two the inductees were re-educated and tested. The testing comprised of emotional, psychological, and physical test to weed-out the true White American Nation from the non-whites and the corrupted. Section Three was the final test. This was the place where true believers were given their third test according to the Reverend Stewardt's instructions.

The theme park was the perfect institution for a re-education camp. There were gun positions at the highest places. Each of the gun crews was equipped with a sniper rifle and an automatic weapon. The sniper rifle was collected from liberated property within the established border of the new nation of Columbia. The instructions to the gun crews were simple: No one escapes! No one resists! No one challenges a true believer! Fire could be called down from those inside the camp who were deemed the 'chosen' or a gun position could exact discipline without request.

Currently, there were over five thousand individuals alive in the camp. Only one hundred and fifty were in section three. While the intentions were similar to the camps ran by the SS in World War Two, the conditions were far different. The sanitation was excellent. There enough bathroom facilities for everyone in the camp and twice that many. Portable showers had been set up near the park's restrooms. All of the concession stands and restaurants were open and operational. Those interned at Camp Columbia were well-fed, clean and even had medical attention.

In another part of the camp, the man stood with a hood on his head and his hands tied roughly behind him. He could hear the sound of the large piece of equipment operating. From the sound and the 'feel' of the operation he sensed the movement of dirt with a track hoe. He only remembered lights and men crashing into his house in Coeur d'Alene, a ride in a van, and then the sounds and smells of a construction site. The hood had been placed over his head and cinched tightly before he left his apartment. He could hear the crunch of boots around him and sensed others nearby. He had prayed continuously since he was taken, but so far Allah had not answered. He remained quiet after his entail questions were answered with a blow to the side of his head.

The man was now lifted to his feet and led to another location. The hands released him and he wavered for a moment, and then stood upright. He heard voices approaching him, but could not make out the words. He felt the presence of others and the sound of clicking and fabric. He then heard the voice, "I am a member of the White American Nation. I am a freedom fighter. The only true humans are white and Christian." The hooded man could not fathom what this was all about. He thought, "This is America—all are equal." He did not feel pain. His body fell immediately to the ground. He did not hear the report of the shot fired into his head. In fact he could not think at all. He was only conscious of his beating heart, his chest raising and lowering, and his legs randomly kicking. Within moments the brilliant white light spread from the center of his vision to the full extent of his optic nerve and then time stopped.

The new W.A.N. inductee was congratulated by the senior educators and provided additional instructions. The inductee grasped the dead non-white and moved him to the pit. He pushed the non-white into the hole and the body landed on others that were partially covered with fresh soil. He would work at this site for another day and then get his assignment in the field. As the young inductee looked around the perimeter of the compound he saw twenty or so pits similar to this one and similar inductees. He was proud that he had made it through the final test and now belonged to something larger than himself. Another hooded victim was led forward and began to speak. The inductee swung the pistol and silenced him. "This was starting to be fun," he thought.

INEL Attack—Arco, Idaho
0645 Pacific Standard Time

Chuck Martin was in charge of security for the Idaho National Engineering Laboratory and was in a living hell. He watched without ability to change the outcome of the mission, talk to subordinates, and activate the laboratories meager air defense or anything else. His mind reeled with questions, "Who? Why? Where from? What did they want?" He found that he had stood and rocked forward on his feet. He had inadvertently pulled his shoulders up willing the aircraft to continue to fly over the base. He thought to himself, "I am going to have some fly boy's ass. This is a restricted facility—no over flights." Another thought came to him, what if this were an exercise to demonstrate the effectiveness of security on the base. Then it would be his ass in a wringer, rather than another's.

Chuck watched in disbelief as the aircraft's bomb bay swung open. His shoulders slumped a bit and the veins protruded from his neck, while his hands gripped his gun tighter. He watched impotent to make any change in the outcome of doomsday.

Stan now temporarily relieved of his role as pilot watched as the target approached. He knew that the Rockeye would soon be deployed, slowed with a drag chute to allow them to get clear of the area and then explode twenty feet above the target sending out hundreds of bomblets that would themselves explode. These bomblets would tear through the drums spilling the contents around the entire area. Some of the contents would be blown as large particles while other would be almost disintegrated to a fine powder.

The Rockeye cleared the bomb bay cleanly. Stan felt the release and Chuck saw the bomb fall from the aircraft and a chute deploy. Both men had the same feeling of anticipation, but both wanted opposite outcome. As soon as the bomb was deployed, Stan took over control of the F-111 and moved it quickly to 400 knots. He did not climb away because he wanted to reduce risk of fragmentation damage. High School physics taught that the line of site decreased as the straight line horizontal distance increased. To lift the aircraft would only make it more susceptible to getting caught in the explosion.

The bomb made a retarded descent while the pressure sensitive trigger came closer and closer to sending the message that would cause it to spring to a short-live life. The bomb reached the preset altitude and exploded causing the hundred or so bomblets to move outward for one, two, three, or four seconds. This allowed the Rockeye to spread destruction over a large area of real estate. However, with a low altitude explosion as this setting called, the three and four second bomblets would actually contact the ground and bounce around before exploding.

When the Rockeye exploded, Chuck actually sat back on his boulder with sagging shoulders in disbelief. From his vantage point it looked like a shotgun blast to the containers. Some containers were still airborne and a cloud of dust rose from the previously ordered stacks. "What in the hell!" he thought. Stan prepared to leave his perch and run to his pickup and hustle back to the laboratory front gate. As he started to climb down the first boulder ledge a siren sounded. Stan looked back and saw the fire truck already pulling from the station. He also noticed that the aircraft was making a leisurely turn to the east. In horror, Stan understood that this guy was setting-up for a second run. The guys from the fire station were almost on site. "What can I do from here?" he thought to himself.

Stan keyed his mike, "Relax for a few; I will get us centered for another approach. What speed do you want this approach to be?"

The bombardier responded, "Make this run at 2-0-0 knots. We need to get the hell out of Dodge when we release this load. It is going to make a big fire, very quickly." Stan continued to move the aircraft to the south to get a good line on the target.

Chuck watched the aircraft in its path. His mind ran through calculations of airspeed, direction and altitude. He found himself mumbling, "Come on. Keep coming. Come around." He knew that it was completely illogical to even think that he could do any damage with his 7mm Magnum, but he had to use whatever he had. The aircraft continued to loiter to the southeast and set-up for his next run.

The F-111 and its deadly load moved with practiced efficiency. The bombardier reset his sights while the pilot made textbook maneuvers for the next run. Out of the corner of bombardier's right eye he saw a fleeting glint from one of the small hillocks to the west. He looked in that direction, but saw nothing else. He thought to himself, "It is just some trash left out in the desert." He returned to his calculations and turned the selector switch to ARM the two incendiary weapons. These bombs were a far cry from the old canisters of napalm used in Viet Nam and wars previous. These were specialized weapons with white phosphorus, an accelerant cocktail, and a thermal sensitive expanding flammable gel. The phosphorus was intended to get the fire started; the accelerant created the initial fire ball, but the real mechanism of the incendiary bomb was the foam. The flammable gel expanded to fifty times its volume and became more flammable as it expanded. A few of the ordinance men from a carrier group got an ounce of the stuff and said that they had a real nice fire that lasted for eight hours. As the fire burned the gel expanded and burned and expanded some more.

Chuck Martin waited. He had already positioned his bipod legs on the largest bolder facing south. He had three rounds next to his 7mm ready to use and was looking at the F-111 through binoculars. He noticed that the bomb bay was still open. Chuck Martin made a choice of first shot, and then started to calculate second and third shot. He waited.

Ramming Speed—Snake River Dam near Bliss, Idaho
0700 Pacific Standard Time
Captain Cummings—Casper—now saw the dam ahead. He had made several practice intercepts on the dam flying wild weasel

practice missions. His ground crew had placed a radar transponder on the dam and their mission was to lock and fire before their Shrike radar was detected. Casper now saw the bomb bay of the F-111 open. "Christ!" he thought. Then out load, "This was going to be fun!" The sarcasm of the last statement did more to prepare Casper for what was coming, rather than fire any false bravado that he might feel. Casper cleared gear from his ejection seat and secured all loose material and pushed the power levers forward.

Bliss Dam was a low head dam which meant that it was a small interruption in the flow of the Snake River. It was a means of flood control and of minor power generation. It was one a string of dams along the Upper Snake. The dividing line between the Upper Snake and the Lower Snake was Hells Canyon Dam. Every dam in the upper Snake River dutifully has a fish ladder built into the original design. The fish ladder at Bliss was of exceptional design and could boast in excess of 99.9% live fish transport both up and down the river. The problem arose when there were only local fish to make the trip. Fish no longer made the trip from the ocean to the upper reaches of the Snake River because of Hells Canyon Dam. The rules for dams came too late for the Snake River salmon.

Alpha flight was three miles from the target. The bombardier had control of the aircraft and the pilot John was looking at the map on the monitor for the next target. A loud warning sounded. John quickly looked at the instruments. He started with the engines and worked through hydraulic and electrical indicators. Then a mechanical voice started to speak, "Collision, pull up. Collision, pull up." This was a new feature in the F-111 since he had flown. He scanned outside his Plexiglas bubble but saw the ground 1000 feet below. He looked to his left, then right. The warning continued.

Casper had performed 'cloud busting over the Pacific whenever he could. The maneuver consisted of three parts. First the Phantom was placed in a sharp climb. Then the power was decreased to idle. Finally, the aircraft stalled and fell vertically until power was reinitialized. He had spent many hours finding a thunderhead, accelerating up the boundary and them nosing over with power at minimum and fell through the cottony white for several seconds. Casper was now in position to make the final move on the other aircraft. Casper held tightly as he flew through the jet wash from the other plane and then pulled back on his power levers.

The pilot and the bombardier both saw the cause of the alarm at the same time and both men took action at the same time. Their cockpit canopy filled with the vision of twin turbines and the rear end of an aircraft. The pilot's hand was on the joystick when the collision occurred. The last sensations sensed by the two F-111 fliers was the screeching sound of tearing metal, wind and flying Plexiglas as their canopy exploded inward and the compression of their body into a very small space.

Casper had lost site of the aircraft but he felt the impact. Just as the impact occurred, he pulled the curtain over his head actuating the ejection seat. The canopy exploded and ejected away from the aircraft. Now the tangle of two aircraft was now starting to separate and fall downward at faster rate than motion in a forward direction. His seat then exploded when the two rocket engines that propelled the seat away from the aluminum coffin. Casper lost consciousness as the weight of ten gravities compressed his organs.

The falling debris that was once aircraft continued to fall toward the ground and the Snake River.

Assault—Spokane, Washington
1155 Pacific Standard Time

The mortars huffed as they left the tube. Unlike the movies, they did not whistle, whine or give much of any warning. Veterans of mortar attacks state that they can 'feel' the mortars coming. The people of Spokane had no warning this bright morning. All of the scouts were busy loading and firing. There was a short pause between each firing as each of the four Scouts rotated the mortar 10 degrees.

The combined effect would be a 360 degree ring of death around the building. The next salvo would start at five degree to the left of the first salvo and repeat the process for nine more rounds. The second salvo would also be slightly closer-in as each scout would elevate his tube ten degrees. Scout One could hear the distant explosions, but had no time to see his handiwork. Hang—Drop—Cover—Reset—Hang.

Suddenly the communication link in his ear crackled, "Rats on the grating." This was a message from Scout Four. Scout Four had the best cover and was responsible for all of the determent processes. The switches to the radio controls that actuated explosive charges were at his location. Scout One keyed his microphone, "Pull the pins."

The Spokane Police Department S.W.A.T. Team was attempting a different access to the roof top. The old gothic building where destruction was being sent forth had external metal fire escapes. The S.W.A.T. team was three floors below the roof top and the squad of five men were carefully moving up the fire escape. The lead S.W.A.T. member heard the clanking, but took a moment to realize what the sound meant as a threat.

When each scout had pulled the cotton close line it pulled the pins from four fragmentation grenades each that had been rigged to drop upon release. Scout Four had seen this work in Baghdad before and after the Gulf Wars. He learned his trade from American and Iraqi fighters. In the former case they were called 'defenders of the people' and in the latter case they were called terrorists. According to whom one was speaking, the terms were interchangeable. The lines with the pins attached flew towards each Scout's position and the grenades began to fall toward the grating of the fire escape.

The lead S.W.A.T. member looked on the grates above him and saw the grenades rolling on topmost level. Several grenades had clanked down to the level above them and several more fell from the grating. The S.W.A.T. leader barked into his microphone, "Grenades, back—back…" The S.W.A.T. team had moved down one level before the first grenade exploded. The S.W.A.T. leader felt the pressure, heat and some fragment impact him just before a secondary set of explosions caused a small vibration and a pinging sound through the metal fabric of the fire escape.

Scout Four smiled when he felt and heard the second set of explosions.

The S.W.A.T. commander on the ground watching the scene from a safe distance said, "Get those men down." He knew that it was already too late. What he saw next would stay with him in nightmares and unguarded moments when fully awake.

Scout Four returned to his mortars and prepared for the second salvo. He neatly aligned nine mortar rockets, reset his elevation, and rotated his mortar five degrees. He would walk the rounds ten degrees in the reverse direction. He did all this as the sound of screeching metal and screaming men came to his ears from the near side of the building.

Scout Four had set his ingenious scenario just right. The hand grenades would most likely do no real damage. These were for shock value and to move the invaders away from the first level. Scout Four thought, "This was a great use of fragmentation grenades. The grenades were used for their shock pressure. Scout Four had rigged a small C-4 shaped charge on each stud and nut that held the fire escape to the building. To this he inserted a pressure-sensitive detonator. When the grenades exploded the pressure activated the detonators and the shaped C-4 literally dissolved the fasteners from the wall. Scout Four was a meticulous man, however. He ran a major shaped charge to the primary landing support five levels down from the roof. Here he used the shaped charge on the support structure and threw in several feet of primer cord to cut the bracing. As explosive surgery went, this was a masterpiece.

The S.W.A.T. leader did not have time to think and less time to communicate. He wrapped arms and legs around the outside major support. Somehow in the next moments he connected his rappelling carabineer to the metal support. He did not have long to wait for the next act of this play.

The S.W.A.T. Commander, one mile from the building mouthed the word, "No!" He watched in horror as the top five or six levels of the fire escape separated from the wall in several puffs of smoke and slowly started to move away from the building. He blinked and wiped the moisture from his eyes. When he looked back through the binoculars, the metal rigging was at a ninety degree angle to the building. The escape remained attached through the entire arc. When it slammed into the building he watched as three of his five men were ejected from the structure and fell the twenty remaining stories to the street below. With a different voice than he had ever used before, he said, "Get those men off the building. Call in rescue. Quick!" He would not mount another attack on this building. He was done as a commander and as a police officer.

Scout Four smiled again as he felt the thump of the staircase against the side of the building. He liked providing people with surprises. He was half way through his second mortar salvo when he heard the earphone erupt again.

TOW—Bangor Submarine Base, Washington
0500 Pacific Standard Time

The hot tub sound started again and another body surfaced twenty feet in front of the bow. This time it was a green fatigue-clad body. One of the Marines assigned to the boat. Buck chewed tighter on his unlit stogy and gave orders, "Get that body secured. Chief, get me plans for this sucker," pointing at the submarine.

Buck felt the presence of the choppers before he heard them. Two Apache gunships and two Blackhawks with a bunch Army Rangers aboard made tactical approaches and landed one hundred yards down the dock. The Major in charge of the Ranger detachment came forward as the Blackhawk helicopters dusted-off and returned to the helicopter pad on the other side of the base. The Apache gunships did not land, but remained as guardian angels zipping random orbiting courses around the Blackhawk's landing zone. The Major looked at

Buck, saw the S.E.A.L. insignia and decided not to salute. He made this choice not out of disrespect, but with the knowledge that the older man was interested in action—not ceremony.

Buck did not greet the Major; he gave orders, "Major, I want a ten man entry team at my beck and call; you lead it. Second, I want snipers targeting every hatch. Third, I want your M-60 on the primary hatch. Finally, I want your best communications guy with me." The Major did not need further orders, he simply replied, "Yes sir."

The Chief Petty Officer returned with the plans for the submarine. Buck looked at the paper and snorted, "Chief, these are from a toy model."

The Chief responded, "The Navy doesn't allow plans for their nuclear submarines hanging around, but these are far too accurate for luck." The Chief continued, "I think these will work for your purposes."

Buck nodded his head, "O.K. where are the bad guys?"

The Chief of the Boat used a felt marker to identify the compartments that were held by the bad guys. He identified the hatch that was welded shut by the crew and where the Lieutenant J.G. was last seen. Buck asked the Chief, "Can we get access to these compartments?" Buck pointed at the control room and the engine compartment. "Sir, we have already tried. They dogged and welded the hatches from the inside. My men are working on it, but it will be a long time before we get through," the Chief concluded. Buck squeezed the bridge of his nose and massaged the tension from his eyes. Then he heard the sound of his next move.

"Chief, you have five minutes to get every one off and away from the sub. Back everyone away at least two-hundred yards and send all but the people you think I will need immediately to the other side of the base." Buck gave orders quickly. He continued, "Ranger." A young soldier stepped forward. "I want one of those Apaches to land within fifty feet of this position, now." The young soldier immediately got on the radio and made the request. No sooner had he lowered his headset that an Apache swooped over and made an abrupt landing.

Buck stopped the Chief in one of his trips around the dock and gave a final order "Chief, contact headquarters and request a Level Five Nuclear Release." The blood from the Chief's face drained and he wiped his lips. He knew what the S.E.A.L. Commander had in mind. The Chief departed without a word.

Buck moved to the Apache that was now at idle. The cockpit and gunner hatches were open. Buck addressed the pilot, "What are you munitions?"

The pilot responded, "Full load of 20mm and sixteen TOW missiles."

Buck continued questioning the young man, "What kind of kick does the TOW have? How much armor will it pierce?"

The younger man looked stunned, "Sir, these missiles were made for tanks, not submarines."

"Answer my question!" Buck barked.

"Sir, the maximum armor piercing effect is 5 inches," the young man replied.

"Son, I am going to paint two spots on that submarine. I want you to place half of your missiles on one spot and the other on the second spot," Buck ordered. The pilot's eyes were wide and he prepared to speak, but Buck cut him off, "I then want you to return to base and rearm."

Buck sent the missile technician with a can of spray paint to mark the spot near the control tower and the missile compartment. He returned in short order. Buck turned and spoke to the Apache pilot with the Ranger's radio, "Sink that sub, son—now!" With little fanfare and no warning, the first TOW exploded and chunks of metal flew against the steel container that Buck and his group crouched behind. When Buck looked over the top of his refuge, he saw that a great deal of metal was lying about and that the asphalt dock surface was on fire in several places. He also heard strange popping and sizzling sounds coming from the direction of the submarine.

Buck spoke over the radio again, "Pour it in. That is an order." With that command the Apache fired one TOW after the other until all of the weapons were expended. The Apache the rose in the air and banked to the east and disappeared.

Buck and his team moved from behind the barrier that had been their refuge and stepped gingerly over metal that was smoking. Smoke covered the entire dock and the wind was so slight that the smoke hung over the submarine. As the smoke cleared Buck first felt horror, then concern. What he saw emerging from the smoke was disconcerting. Buck spit out the well chewed cigar, reached in his pocket, and stuck a fresh one in his mouth.

DE-BARBING THE TRIDENT—
CHAPTER 7

Retreat—Pend d'Oreille River near Cusick, Washington
0100 Pacific Standard Time

Sam did not duck or attempt to find cover. He did not try because he was not prone to hiding from his enemy and the boat was far too small to provide cover. The boat operator immediately rotated the motor control to full throttle. The boat also started a zigzag course that was irregular. The boat driver also started to make for a small cove on the opposite shore. A second shot sounded, but no impact was detected. This time those in the boat saw the location of the muzzle flash. The boat driver saw Sam raise his automatic weapon and maintained a steady straight course. Sam discharged a full clip in the general direction of the muzzle flash.

Ten seconds after the sound of the second round, Sam was sure that he had not been hit. He said in a clear voice, "Report." Like a well oiled machine his contingent began to count off, "One, Two, Three Dead, Four Hit, Five Dead, Six, Seven Dead."

Becker questioned Number Five, "Five, where are you hit."

Number Five responded in a voice that clearly denoted pain, "I took a round in the vest, Sir. I don't know if it penetrated, but I have a broken rib—for sure." Sam instructed one of the other men to watch the injured man and make sure that he did not go into shock or become unconscious.

The boat grounded against the East shore. The men of the crew began to move quickly to load the gear and prepare to pack out. Sam gave them instruction, "Take your time. We are in friendly territory. Take good care of our dear." Sam heard a rustle to his left. Like a cat he swung to meet the new threat.

A voice rang out from the dark, "Knife, this is Eagle Eye—coming in." Sam responded, "Come on in Eagle Eye." Eagle Eye was their cover. Eagle Eye gave his report, "Only two shots, Sir. I had no joy and didn't waste a round." Eagle Eye then looked down and saw his dead comrades. He thought, "This was not supposed to happen, damn!"

Sam had not considered being run out of an attack. He and the other units had had their way with the sheep on the other side of the river. He believed that he and his cause were invincible. The reality of death and failure now was on his mind and in his vocabulary. He suddenly flinched as he unconsciously thought of the leather belt impacting his naked calves. His grandfather wielding the straps and his father held his shoulders during this correction activity. He could still hear his father reply the word 'amen' every time his grandfather made the point about failure and supremacy and faith in the white race. His legs jerked uncontrollably for a moment. Sam's face hardened and he returned his mind to the present.

The team loaded their gear, secured their dead, and departed the scene. On the way back to headquarters, Sam rehearsed his report that he would soon give to the Reverend-General. He thought again to himself, "How many more gunners are on the other side of the river?" As he traveled along the winding road to the compound, his mind oscillated between the possibility of failure and the surety of domination.

Pest Control—Spokane, Washington
1315 Pacific Standard Time

"Inbound!" crackled through the earpiece of each of the four men on the rooftop. Each one began to scan the sky. Scout One continued, "Northeast, high approach contrail. Get the Stinger up." The Stinger was an anti-aircraft hand held missile system that was used by all of the world's armies and terrorist in one version or another. Scout One saw his man at the northeast corner raise the tube and took aim.

The twenty-five year old Air Force Captain sat in the padded office chair watching the 30 inch monitor. Flight information scrolled across the sides of the view while the heads-up display provided a clear view of the surrounding area. As he moved his head the view changed accordingly. If he wanted to configure his screen so that drop-down windows showed various views, he could. He toggled a switch on his flight control mounted on his right armrest. The view zoomed 400%. At four miles he could see the sweat forming on each man's face. The young Captain had logged over two thousand hours, but had never left the ground. The common joke in his command was that he had more combat flight experience than most pilots and did not have a set of wings on his uniform front. The young Captain jolted when the loud voice disturbed his virtual world.

"Holy mother!" said the Colonel who stood behind the chair and watched the monitor. The full bird continued, "It looks like there are four of them. If only I had a Strike eagle ready for a mission."

The Captain spoke haltingly, "Sir, uhmm, Gracie is, uhmm, armed."

The Colonel bellowed, "What! Who the hell is Gracie?"

The Captain lowered his head a bit and replied, "Gracie is the Predator U.A.V. that is inbound on the target, sir." The Captain's backbone gained calcification and he continued, "Colonel, I have eight Hellfire missiles that I can place within 50 cm of a target. Do you want these men killed?" The Colonel stared for a moment. Gracie's operator flipped another toggle on the joystick and a weapons indicator appeared on the monitor. The Captain and the Colonel saw the man in his sight begin to send mortars into the city again.

The Colonel barked, "Take him out and then the others; Now!"

The Captain rotated the selector switch on his left armrest and depressed the trigger on the joystick. The image appeared a bit milky as the imaging software compensated for the flare of the missile motor blasting toward the target. The young Captain kept the laser designator at the foot of the target. Suddenly his target moved. The Captain panned back to get a better view and saw that the man had a Stinger on his shoulder and was trying to get a target lock. The Captain placed the target designator on the man's mid-section and waited. He watched as the man selected through the targeting mode of the Stinger without success. The Predator was stealthy and had advanced active electronic counter measure technology that most combat aircraft lacked. The Captain was not worried about the Stinger.

Scout One watched as the contrail of the missile came closer and closer. "Why didn't the other man shoot?" he questioned. He looked again and lost the contrail which meant that it was close to impact. He curled into a protective position behind the large potted plant, sucked-in all the air he could hold and waited.

The video screen returned to the milky vision again and the Captain rolled the zoom back to be able to take in the entire rooftop in the view of his monitor. The northeast corner was gone. The roof was afire and much of the retaining wall was gone. He watched as the area near the northwest of the roof erupted in explosion. He got a 'two-for'; the ammunition from the northwest corner was exploding and killed bad guy number two.

Scout One was stunned. His hearing was gone and he was burned in several places on his legs. He looked through the smoke and saw only flame in the northeast corner and was rocked by the mortars popping-off in the northwest. His mind started to function again and he asked himself, "Where did that come from?"

The Captain turned the selector on the left armrest to a symbol that looked like a capitol 'E'. The symbol, sigma, indicated the shoot and forget mode. He would line-up the target designator, depress his trigger and the Hellfire would go to that point. Then he would select the next and so on. The Captain had selected five places on the rooftop and depressed his trigger. Five Hellfire missiles were on their way. He sat back in his seat and focused on counter measures and straight and level flight. The Colonel interrupted the Captain's work, "What is happening?"

The Captain replied, "Sir, Gracie is twenty seconds from taking off the top of that building."

The Colonel said, "Let's see!"

Scout One was moving toward his Stinger and opened the fiberglass case. He looked up to the sky to the northeast and froze. He saw several small contrails heading toward his location. He did not continue his set-up for the Stinger. He sat on the rooftop and gave a small salute and closed his eyes.

The Battle—Idaho-Washington State Line
0800 Pacific Daylight Time

The last vehicle in line took another hit and rocked back and began to teeter. As the smoke began to clear he saw Jones, one of his R.O.T.C. kids, pushing the vehicle back on its side and his comrades piling sandbags under the near side to help stabilize the rig. Everyone teased Jones for building his muscles to incredible proportions. He was always in training for the Strongman Competition and now that training paid off. The vehicle was reset and Jones looked the way of the Sergeant and gave him a thumbs-up signal and kneeled and began once again to fire.

Sergeant Bavairo turned to make a call to the sniper, but saw that the young lieutenant was already on that call. He overheard the young officer make the correct call. "Sniper One, disable the recoilless rifle on the pick-up immediately. Use any means necessary." Bavairo watched through his high tech binoculars and switched them to infrared. He watched as the first round of the sniper rifle ricocheted-off of the bus. He grabbed the Bat Phone, "Sniper One, do you have a shot at the barrel near the breach?"

The response was nearly immediate, "Roger, good shot—O.K.—You bet we do. Standby."

Bavairo returned to his field glasses. His infrared image showed a hot spot where the breach met the barrel or the recoilless rifle.

Suddenly the barrel had a hotter than normal spot just in front of the breach. Spotter One had loaded an armor piercing shell and blew a hole in the barrel of the rifle. As Bavairo watched, the barrel and breach erupted into a bloom of heat as the round wedged in the damaged barrel and exploded within the chamber. The gun was out of commission.

Bavairo switched back to standard optics in time to see the gunner jump over the bed of the Toyota and receive a large caliber round in the middle of his gut. He would live for about ten minutes in excruciating pain. The shot was selected to give the recipient the cruelest of deaths. He thought to himself that he was very glad that the sniper was on their side. He looked through his scope again at the enemy who lay on the ground. He held his mid-section and appeared to be trying to plug the hole left by the large caliber sniper round. Bavairo did not smile or nod in affirmation, the soldier heart felt no remorse or joy—only duty. His warrior mind moved to the next task at hand.

Without any notice, the vehicles at the rear of the column began to reverse their direction and move up the highway toward Coeur d'Alene. The mortars reset their aim and made short work of two of the three remaining vehicles. Bavairo heard the 'woof' sound from both mortar pits. "Good," he thought. Pit One was manned and back in action. The last vehicle was disabled by carefully placed rounds from Sniper One.

The young officer crouching near Bavairo continued to make commands. The Sergeant heard the Lieutenant order the mortars to concentrate on the Bradley Fighting Vehicle. Thirty seconds after the order, mortar rounds started to fall all around the Bradley and turning it into an inferno. The rear of the vehicle came open and seven men ran quickly east.

The order from the young officer to the mortar crews was to fire as far east as possible to prevent any of the attackers from escaping. Bavairo heard the report of the sniper rifles every twenty to thirty seconds. He knew that each round was another attacker dead. There were no further incoming rounds and Bavairo acted, "Squad Three follow me." He then turned to the other men, "Keep careful lookout for any unfriendly, but keep the aim off of the squad." After he gave this command he heard the order being relayed down the line.

Bavairo made hand signals to two of the members of squad three to move out in front of the squad to reconnoiter. The two men jumped over the overturned vehicle barrier and began to move onto the bridge. After the point men had crossed the bridge and set-up on the east side, they both made the hand signals for the squad to advance. The squad looked to Bavairo, who made the signal to move in standard leap frog fashion across the bridge. The sniper's long rifles continued to fire. Bavairo was the first man to enter the killing zone. As he came around the rear of the Bradley vehicle a man turned and raised a weapon in his direction. He placed three neatly spaced rounds into his chest. Bavairo and three of squad members moved cautiously to the bus.

"Damn! Please, no," one of the R.O.T.C. soldiers worded. Bavairo followed his gaze and shook his head in sadness. He thought for a moment of finding every wounded enemy and makes them suffer a slow and tortuous death for what he beheld, but no. He was an American Soldier.

Orders—White American Nation Compound near Bunker, Idaho

0619 Pacific Standard Time

Sam reported to the Reverend-General. He gave a clear report, including his concern over his near loss to a woman. The General took in the information and started to plan a tactical change to the insurgency operation. Then without a change in the man, Reverend Stewardt emerged and placed his hand on the larger man's shoulder. He looked Sam straight in the eye and said, "Brother Becker, this is no more than a test that God has chosen for you. You are the finest Christian Soldier that I have in this army of God; do not doubt yourself," Reverend Stewardt concluded. The General returned, "Major Becker, take your crack team to this location." He pointed to a red dot on a topographic map. "Report has it that there are a group of non-whites who have established a defensive compound. I agree that it is time to 'take-the-gloves-off'." The General came to full stature and said in a commanding voice, "Major Becker you have your hunting license. Cleanse the west shore and take no prisoners. Any who resist—eliminate." Sam Becker smiled and thought again of his grandfather and the Becker litany.

Sam departed the command center while the General looked at the situation board that consumed an entire wall of the bunker and shook his head in concern. Prong 2 had not reported and it was the most important for the continuation of his new homeland and the White American Nation.

Punchout—Snake River Dam near Bliss, Idaho
0730 Pacific Standard Time

Casper regained consciousness just in time to feel the hard jerk from his opening parachute. He looked through his feet at the falling wreckage. The training and the NATOPS (Naval Aviation Tactical Operations Procedures) manual was correct, the ejection seat pushed the pilot up and away from the wreckage. The two aircraft were smoking and taking slightly different paths to the ground. As he watched, the F-111 crashed on the north shore of the Snake River about one-half mile below the dam. His Phantom crashed downstream in the middle of the river. Another explosion erupted from the F-111 crash site as the armed bombs 'cooked-off' from the fire. He quickly scanned the area and saw no other chutes. He could only conclude that the other pilots did not punch-out in time. He had little remorse.

The Snake River near Bliss was a deep canyon with small side canyons that led to the plain above. This portion of the Snake River Plateau was dedicated to raising potatoes, grains, and fresh rainbow trout for the world. Bliss was a very small off ramp on Interstate 84 that traversed the southern portion of Idaho. The area was rugged and peopled by rugged individuals. While most were familiar with fighter aircraft in their skies, few appreciated the jet jockeys disturbing their boring lives.

Casper now began to evaluate his own situation. The wind was drifting him toward the dam. It appeared that he would end up getting wet. The training manual on the Phantom emergency equipment that the direction of drift after ejection and appropriate deployment could be modified by pulling on one side or the other of the primary harness straps. Casper pulled on the left strap and nothing happened. He pulled on the right, nothing happened. Casper thought to himself, "So much for the manual." He calculated that he had about another 30 seconds before landing. It looked more and more like he would end up in the water and that he would end up just above the dam or just below.

He watched as several pickup trucks from a nearby field were moving down the road toward the burning carcass of the F-111. As he watched, another one of the onboard munitions exploded. The trucks stopped and reversed their course. His gaze returned to the dam and his most likely landing area. He weighed his options. If he landed above the dam in the lake would the suction from turbines suck his chute and him through the dam? How would he get out of the water even if he could ditch the chute? He had little time to contemplate his chances as the dam and the water was quickly approaching. It was then that he saw the greatest threat to his life, the exposed power lines and transformer nodes near the powerhouse. Like a zoom on a camera his vision conjured-up hitting one of those live circuits and frying like moth in a bug zapper.

A gust of wind pushed the canopy and made him swing wildly. Out of the corner of his eye he saw a glint from a vehicle window. He tried to twist in that direction enough to see what caused the reflection. He saw a man in blue work coveralls standing next to a pickup truck. He held something in his right hand that he brought to this shoulder. Casper verbally prayed, "O Lord, don't let that guy shoot me." He waved his arms and shouted as loud as he could, "U.S. Navy. I am a good guy." Casper thought how stupid that sounded. He saw the man lower the gun and run to the powerhouse. The man had only been using the gun's scope as a vision aid.

Casper returned his attention to his landing spot. The ground was mere feet away. He was heading for the lake above the dam. He pulled on his left strap with all his might and felt the canopy give away a bit in his hands. He started to swing to the left. The ground seemed to be coming-up far faster than he planned. He bent his knees and braced for landing. The landing was incredible. He hit and rolled.

When he again looked around he found that he was standing on the top of the dam. He had rolled and come up standing on top of the dam looking upstream. He was thanking God and contemplating his good fortune when the straps pulled taught at his shoulders. Before he could unclasp the quick release buckles on the harness he was being pulled over the edge of the dam's service walkway where he had landed. He swung in the harness in time to see the wires and transformers in the power distribution station directly below him. He looked around to see if there was anything he could do. He was still thinking this as his feet left the edge of the concrete skirt at the top of the dam. He felt his feet slip off the edge and begin their plummet downward as he swung below the still filled canopy.

Sinking—Bangor Submarine Base, Washington
0500 Pacific Standard Time

The sound of the Apache rotors diminished and the smoke began to dissipate. Buck and his crew peered through the smoke. Each man inhaled and choked on the smoke that still rose from the burning asphalt. The wharf and service area showed the aftermath of a rocket attack. What could burn was aflame and what could not burn was hot to the touch. As Buck took in this 'Hell on earth', he felt ashamed that his pulse raced and the warrior in him cried for more. The warrior in

Buck demanded more destruction and greater fire power, but then the officer inserted responsibility and demanded consideration. The eternal conflict within Buck continued.

Buck quickly analyzed the situation. A hole about the size of a hub cap was drilled through the side of the submarine. Steam was rolling from the opening as well smoke from the interior. His major question was to answer the burning question (no pun intended) about the fissionable material.

The submarine still sat in the same position in its mooring. It was not tilted or in any other way affected by the bombardment except for the smoke, steam and the whole in the side. Buck thought that as much fire power that he had unleashed would have clearly blown the sub apart, but it only 'holed' it and made a mess inside. Any other man would have thought of what he had just done and had second thoughts, but Buck was ready and steady. He took a stand, made a decision and moved to the next decision. Buck had the beginnings of a plan, now to put it into action.

Inside the missile room of the submarine, SSBN Kentucky, there was little time to contemplate a next move or for that matter time for any thought at all. Anyone who has survived the surprise attack within a submarine, an aircraft in flight, or in a tank on land, will tell the story of the attack as a feeling of incredible pressure, loss of sensation, and then awakening some time later. Collectively, those who have survived an overwhelming attack will tell the listener that they did not hear a concussion, feel heat, or see flame. What they will tell you is that there was a split second of complete isolation and a sense of forsakenness. The men working in the missile room in fact felt a microsecond of forsakenness prior to their death by shrapnel, pressure wave, and heat. All of the invaders in SSBN Kentucky were dead and the missile room was not a place for human beings or any other living creatures. The submarine's missiles again were under control of the United States Navy and therefore the President of the United States.

Buck spoke to the man with the radiation suit that arrived during the bombardment by the Apache, "Go check for radiation. Do not put yourself at risk. We may still have unfriendlies inside the sub." The man pulled his radiation suit closures yet tighter and gingerly made his way to the submarine. Buck watched as he carefully skirted the perimeter of the hole and quickly took a look inside. The man in the radiation suit returned quickly to the minimal protection of the barrier that Buck and his crew used as a shield.

Buck spoke before the man had a chance to report. "How hot?" was Buck's question.

The man saw that Buck was a no-nonsense officer and answered directly, "Men can work for 15-20 minutes in close proximity without permanent damage, but need to clear out soon after completely away from the scene." The man continued, "Sir, there is something else. There is a pretty good fire still cooking those missiles." The man did not have to finish his report; Buck knew what had to be done next.

At the atomic level, the Plutonium 239 was doing what it always did. As the atomic particles in the 4.5667 Kilograms shed neutrons, protons and electrons in the normal decay process, radiation in the form of gamma radiation, beta particles, and alpha particles is emitted at high rates. In the normal nuclear weapon, these particles were absorbed and retained within the bomb casing with a carbon modulator casing and a thin lead casing.

Missiles tubes 1, 3 and 5 had sustained damage and several of the warheads within those missile tubes had ruptured casings. The narrow crack in the bomb casing and the missile skin allowed deadly radiation to escape. The alpha particle made up of two neutrons and two protons were easily blocked by paper or cloth. The beta particles made up of high speed free electrons required aluminum or a similar material to prevent tissue residence. However, the most deadly, the gamma radiation was in wave pulse form and could penetrate four inches of concrete or one-half inch of lead. This was the feared radiation of those who chose to work around high energy physics and the death of Madam Curie.

The radiation continued to emit from the opening and would continue at a lesser and lesser rate for the next 300,000 years. In the next 300,000 years the amount of Plutonium 239 would reduce by half of its mass every 24,390 years. It would finally diminish to a point, around 1.5 grams of the original critical mass, where it would resemble slightly higher than normal background radiation levels. 300,000 years was far too long to wait.

In the next ten minutes Buck ordered the cement mixer trucks from the local job site on base and all of the cellulose insulation material available near the base. In addition to these requisitions, he had the dock master and his engineering crew begins to rig a temporary patch with access of a four inch fire line and a one inch one way vent.

As Buck continued to chew on his cigar, he thought about time. Would he have enough?

230-Grains—Arco, Idaho
0710 Pacific Standard Time

Bravo flight, one of two F-111Bs hijacked from Mountain Home Air Force base, had turned to make a second run against the first nuclear reactor facility in the United States. The pilot and bombardier sat next to each other in the cockpit. The first run had fragmented the storage containers and made a mess of the area. The Rockeye bomlets shredded the containers of nuclear waste like a shotgun blast. The pilot could see vehicles arriving to the location. He was silently impressed with the response time. Then his mind hardened and he thought of the elevated initial body count when he released his next ordinance.

The selector switch was set on arm for the two 750-pound Mark 77 air dropped incendiary munitions. Each bomb carried 110 gallons of kerosene and benzene fuel. The pilot smiled when he thought about the press release from the pentagon that the Mk-77 was superior to the older gasoline napalm weapons and was safer to the environment.

The F-111B had almost completed its downwind turn and the pilot was readying the aircraft for bombardier control. The Bravo flight pilot was thinking about his next targets. His secondary targets were the dams at and below Twin Falls, Idaho and the highway bridge at Twin Falls. He knew that his flight was a diversion, but it did not matter. He was inflicting harm to the enemy. "Amen!" he thought.

Chuck Martin vision began to blur as he watched the aircraft through his binoculars. It was then he realized that he wasn't blinking or breathing. He began to do both after his brain registered the oversight. Chuck was mad, but he quickly put that aside. He focused again on the open bomb bay of the aircraft. As he kept the binoculars to his eyes he started running through the mathematics of two-dimensional motion in his head. If the aircraft was approaching then any error would be magnified by the combined speed of both his bullet and the plane.

However, if he fired as the aircraft was passing over or opening from his location then any error would be marginalized. He lowered his binoculars and situated himself behind the boulder in direct line to the reactor building. He lowered himself as much as possible and used the bipod legs to scan the sky. "This was a decent set-up." he thought.

The sound of the twin turbines grew louder and he could now smell the jet exhaust from the previous run. He performed hundreds of trigonometric functions in his head. He remembered the two dimensional vector problems from his high school physics class. He did these calculations as he watched the first of the emergency response vehicles roll-up to the burning near reactor number one. All of these calculations and thoughts took only a moment. He rolled his fingers that were wrapped around the stock to get blood flowing again. He waited.

COLLAPSE—CHAPTER 8

Counter Attack—Coeur d'Alene, Idaho
1515 Pacific Standard Time

There was not a coordinated effort in the counter attack. It began slowly and moved throughout the population. In years that followed the attack, people of Coeur d'Alene would speak of the counter attack as a mentality of refusal and of what a few dedicated people could accomplish.

The stronghold of the Coeur d'Alene invasion was the Idaho National Guard Armory. Reports began to be heard from remote groups that resistance was being encountered. What bothered the Major in charge of the Idaho take-over most were the units who were not answering the call or making their mandatory check-in. The Major swore to himself and readied himself to call all of the remote operators into the nest. This meant that he was unable to control his area of responsibility. He turned to instruct the radio operator to make contact with the Bunker. He needed to tell the General what was transpiring and ask for help. Before he could mouth the words concrete shards began to pop-up from the floor near the window. "What the Hell!" exploded the young Major. This was not going to happen. A bunch of backwoods 'sheep' were not shooting at his command and daring to think that they could lay siege to him.

The Major gave orders to execute the plan that he had briefed his troops at the beginning of the mission. Men moved to secure sites; moved metal shutters over windows and moved to sniper positions on the roof. The Major could hear the single shots from deer rifles and the return of automatic weapons. The major felt very safe. He had superior fire power and the armory was built like a fort. The Major then sensed something had changed. He no longer heard the two-part exchange of fire, but a steady cacophony of automatic and large caliber weapons. The deer hunters had automatic and heavy weapons. This was unexpected, much unexpected.

The explosion on the roof knocked dust and plaster into the armory rooms below. The Major asked the radio operator if he had made contact with the Bunker. The man with the headphones only shook his head. The Major picked up the phone and heard no tone in the headset. He was beginning to feel a shiver of fear creep into his mind.

It was a rough ride on the asphalt street leading to the armory, but Hector Rodriguez guided the D-10 Caterpillar Dozer with purpose. He had watched his uncle, aunt and three cousins taken from their homes and loaded into buses. He knew that he would probably not see them again. The dozer turned toward the entrance to the armory and heard the ping of bullets hitting the large U-blade of the dozer that was lifted in the air to protect the cab. He looked behind and saw three other large dozers making a beeline for the building. His dozer suddenly lurched backwards and he felt heat and pressure engulf the cab.

Inside the armory the Major felt the vibrations from heavy equipment before he could see the earth movers. The major immediately ordered attack with rocket-propelled grenades and concentration on the dozer by snipers. He heard the first RPG explode and felt some relief, but he continued to feel the vibrations and sensed that they were growing stronger. It was then that he peered through the metal shutters and saw not one dozer, but four. Each dozer moved with purpose and cause. He had little time to think.

Hector was furious. He was not physically injured, but he was more committed than ever. He saw that seven men with guns were behind his machine and were following him into the armory. None of the men were dressed alike. One man had on a flowery shirt and sandals while another had full camouflage field gear. He also noticed that most colors and races were represented. Hector's dozer hit the large metal door of the armory and he increased power while his transmission geared down for the contest of wills. Like most operators of heavy equipment, Hector's grasp increased and he gripped the steering handles with increasing force as if he could personally push the door down. The battle between the dozer and the door was short and one-sided. The door blew down, trapping several of the defenders under the door. Hector could hear the screams as his dozer mounted the horizontal door and began to move into the office spaces. The riflemen and women moved quickly into the armory and all of the defenders from the White American Nation were dead or wounded and captured.

The Major slowly came to his senses. He felt the dripping of fluid on his face and reflexively wiped the fluid away. His vision began to clear and he tried to stop the throbbing of his head. The Major thought, "What was his radio operator doing in the air above him?" His vision continued to clear and he realized that his hands and feet were bound with nylon ties. He watched something fall toward his face and then felt the impact. It was then he tasted the unmistakable metal-tinted tang of blood. His radio operator, obviously dead, was being secured to a lamp pole.

The bucket from the fire truck allowed easy access to this posting. A man next to him spoke to him and said, "I don't know who hung the first ones, but the idea caught on quick." The man slapped a pistol against the Major's shoulder and continued, "First, they were hung by the neck, but we lost a few when the head popped-off." The Major moved his mouth as to speak, but was interrupted by the man, "Don't worry, we only hang the dead ones. We want it to be a message— Don't screw with Coeur d'Alene."

The Major thought, "It wasn't supposed to be this way. The sheep were not supposed to have teeth." The Major laid his head against the deck of the ladder truck as it stopped under another light pole.

Tailrace—Snake River Dam near Bliss, Idaho
0735 Pacific Standard Time

Casper began to pray again and invoke any karma that he may have collected over the past years. When the canopy swung him around again he saw the transformer station below and the turbulent tailrace below the dam. Casper clinched his teeth and remembered what his training from D.W.S.T. (Deep Water Survival Training) taught him so many years ago. He had been twenty years old when he left the dock side at North Island Naval Air Station and spent the day being towed by his parachute harness behind a boat, dropped forty feet into the ocean and picked-up and dumped several more times until he landed on the beach. His training continued for another two weeks and involved S.E.R.E. (Survival Evasion Resistance and Escape) School. This entire trip down memory lane took only one second. He remembered the tales of aviators who had successfully ejected only to be pulled under and drowned when their parachute filled with water and currents towed their hapless victims to their doom.

This churning current of water came from the turbines and inherently was a violent place. The current in the tailrace could pull him down and keep him under for longer than he could hold his breath or could scrape him along the bottom of the river and turn him into hamburger. His mind still working on the training caused his hands to move to the quick release snaps just above each shoulder. He spoke to himself as the training memory downloaded into his frontal cortex, "Do not release the quick release snaps until your feet touch a surface; the ground is often farther away than it seems. When your feet make contact quickly lift the quick release mechanism on the right shoulder snap and rock you body the right. This will release the right snap. To release the left quick release snap repeat the release sequence while pulling on the canopy strap above the snap with the left arm." This mental dialog took only milliseconds, but reactivated muscle memory from training so long ago. Casper thought to himself once again, "I could be on the back nine with the guys right now."

119

Casper looked up to his canopy and saw that it was only partially filled with air and was causing him to violently sway like a piñata at his kids birthday party. He looked down and once again saw the top of the transformers with megawatts of electricity awaiting his fall. The image of a bug zapper came into his mind and he unconsciously pulled his legs a little closer to his body.

His body swung again and he could see churning water below him once again. Then his feet hit a cable and he prepared for the inevitable.

Bad day—Idaho-Washington State Line
0843 Pacific Standard Time

Sergeant Bavairo kept keen senses as his men took positions to secure the assault area. As hard as he could try, he could not keep from looking over his shoulder at the people who were the human armor of the lead bus. Each had been handcuffed of tied with a nylon tie to welded loops on the side of the bus. Their feel had been attached similarly against the bus but resting on a piece of metal that protrude from the bus. This arrangement allowed the victims to remain standing and fully engaged as the traveled down the road to the meeting at the bridge.

A sound from the bus caught his ear. One of those who were attached to the bus was still alive, but how, he thought. Bavairo quickly made signs for two more squads and the medics to cross the bridge. Members of the first squad had established a perimeter. As the two squads arrived he gave orders for one squad to reinforce the perimeter and check all combatants for weapons and signs of life. He turned to the squad leader of the third squad and gave the young man specific instructions, "You and the medics release every hostage from the bus and treat if possible." He continued, "You make sure that they are treated with the greatest respect. After all of the hostages are cut down and treated, then check out surviving bad guys." He finished with the reality check, "You read me!" The young corporal nodded his head and grunted. The medics needed no orders, they were already checking for life at the bus.

What Bavairo saw would last him a lifetime of nightmares. Each of the hostages had been stabbed or sliced in the belly. Intestines and gore stretched from open flesh, sometimes spilling to the ground. Several of the soldiers of the third squad were on all fours puking their guts out on the sandy soil of North Idaho.

Bavairo heard the sniper rifles and mortars go silent. He keyed his mike and said, "Report."

The response was from the young Lieutenant, "Sergeant, all of the bad guys are down. I am sending squad to insure all of those who are down are noncombatant living or combatant dead."

Bavairo responded, "Lieutenant, request to lead that patrol."

Bavairo could hear the negative response with the explanation that he was ordered to report to the temporary headquarters at the weigh station two miles down the road.

As he was heading across the bridge, he met the squad that would be beating the bushes. He gathered the young men around him and gave them a briefing, "Treat this as a hostile engagement. No man is down until he is unarmed, dead or shackled. Use the leap from and maintain cover for advances. Watch for booby traps. If a weapon is raised do not hesitate to take-down the target. No one gets hurt on this sweep. Copy?" The men all responded as one, "Yes Sergeant."

Bavairo crossed the bridge and began his walk to the temporary headquarters. All the time he rubbed his eyes as if he could remove the images. As he stepped over the barrier on the Washington side of the bridge, Sniper One bounded over the concrete barrier like a hurdler. He had a medical bag, but no weapon. He looked rather odd running in his Gilly Suit. Bavairo knew where he was going and what he hoped the young man would find. As he looked up and down the line he saw these boys of his helping one another with minor wounds, policing spent casings, and re-reinforcing the barrier. Several were cleaning weapons and loading magazines. These college boys were now seasoned soldiers. The veteran Sergeant walked a little straighter and held his head a bit higher and kept the tears from falling until he was well down the road.

Stabilizing—Bangor Submarine Base, Washington
1700 Pacific Standard Time

The venerable Chief of the Boat was a deep water sailor from the time that he enlisted over forty-three years prior. He had been before the review board twice to challenge mandatory retirement. His first submarine commander, now a three star admiral, always sat at the rear of the hearing making his presence known by adjutants that came to and from the hearing room. The most conspicuous overt endorsement from the admiral was not when he arrived prior to the beginning of the hearing, but when the hearing board was seated. He would walk to where the Chief was standing and give a brisk salute to the enlisted man before the chief could salute him. After the salute came the handshake and the tap on the right shoulder by the admiral's free hand. A head nod at the convening authorities and the admiral took his place in the rear of the room. When the hearing was complete, the admiral would quietly leave the hearing room without comment or indication of approval.

The chief recalled when he and the admiral were in a fight for their lives and the lives of the crew. Their attack boat had just prosecuted a Soviet Boomer and making noise to let the other guy know that he was dead, if this was a real boat. This was during the "'Cold War', my ass," thought the Chief. As they made noise, the commander gave the order for fleet speed and to veer off from the six-o'clock position of the Russian boomer and make for a new contact to the Northeast. The collision came just as the passive sonar detected a close target. In the after action report, it was determined that the Boomer Skipper had ordered full reverse on his right screw and full ahead on the left screw and moved the rudder to starboard. This resulted in the submarine turning on its axis to starboard. At the same time the Boomer skipper called to ascend in the water column 10 meters. When the Chief's attack boat veered-off and made for a new contact, the drove right into the keel, amidships of the much larger Boomer. The collision almost ripped the sail from the attack boat and cause flooding through that access and the many tubes that held periscopes, antennae, and wiring.

The control room was flooding quickly and many of the crew were either incapacitated or busy working to stop leaks. The commander of the boat was working on the periscope and favoring a broken arm and gash on the back of his head. When the Chief looked at him, his eyes said, "Help me Chief." The Chief sprang into action. He ordered the hatches throughout the ship to be set to Condition Zulu. This meant that closed hatches would be 'dogged', locked closed from both sides, and that open hatches would be closed and dogged. The next thing the Chief ordered was to increase the air pressure in the control room to keep the flooding at bay and to aid in damage control efforts.

With the flooding coming under control and pumping removing water, the commander and Chief worked together to stabilize and surface the boat. After the boat was surfaced and all of the procedures had been followed and completed, the commander met with the Chief and thanked him for his leadership. The incident was classified Top Secret and the Chief never mentioned it again. Even when the commander, years later, wanted to thank the Chief for his help, the Chief acted as if he did not know what the commander was speaking about. The commander, know Admiral, was appreciative of the Chief and his support when he needed it the most.

The Chief returned to present.

As the Chief approached the guy who just 'holed' his boat, he began to size him up. He had fought many men in his years and knew that he could still take care of ninety percent of the sailors that he met and all of the 'gyrines', army and air force pukes. But this guy had a 'don't mess with me' look about him. He would listen first, and then make up his mind to beat the living crap out of this guy.

The Chief of the boat appeared at Buck's side. His face was a mask of anger and the tendons in his neck spoke of the control that he was attempting to manage. "Sir, what the hell did you do to my boat?" asked the old salt.

Buck looked him square in the eye without bravado or challenge, "Chief, I saved one million people. Don't you think that that was truly the purpose all along?" The Chief began to relax and understood the decision. As quickly as the two formidable men met in conflict, they now cooperated for success.

"Chief, how much water under the keel?" asked Buck.

The Chief thought for just a moment and said, "They load us in here pretty tight in here. I bet you that there is not more than ten to twelve feet at low tide." Buck chewed his disintegrating cigar. Both men turned around and looked up the far end of the wharf when the backup alarm from the first cement mixer truck arrived. The Chief looked at Buck, narrowed his eyes, and commented, "I think I get your drift, I can help to maintain access after she is on the bottom." Buck looked at the man who was his age and his experience. Both nodded at one another and the Chief left to do his part of the mission.

Men were now climbing all over the submarine. All were suited-up for radiation hazard and were grinding the jagged opening of the hole to make it an appropriate seat for the patch. He watched as the engineering crew fashioned the metal patch and installed the couplers that would allow access to the missile bay. The Lieutenant grade Dock Master approached Buck in a run, "Sir, we have the patch ready. It should do just fine with some sealant." Buck eyed the Dock Master and began to phrase a question, but the Lieutenant beat him to it, "Sir we have been applying lead sealant paint used in the reactor rooms to the inside and outside. When we put the patch on, we should be pretty radiation tight. I have also taken the liberty of getting the radiation blankets we use when working on a reactor core. We will lay these over the areas where men are working and get the count down to near background."

Buck just nodded and said, "Carry on Lieutenant."

Buck was always amazed at the caliber of people that the Navy attracted. This Lieutenant could make a whole lot of money for some company somewhere, but was making the Navy his career. He needed to remember this the next time he ran into one of the bureaucrats in uniform that he tolerated so poorly.

His plan was coming together. He watched as the patch was moved into place and the dogged into place with the contrived rig. Soon the men were scurrying over the submarine hull placing blankets over the patch and the surrounding deck area. Again the sailor with the radiation meter moved toward the sub and clearly took readings and recorded measurements. He turned to Buck and gave a thumbs-up signal.

The sailors with the four inch line and the concrete pump moved into the area adjacent to the wharf and moved the cement mixer to position. Buck saw men on the rear of the mixer pouring bags of cellulose insulation into the mixer with the load of cement. Buck knew that when the salvage job on this boat began, he would get a box of cigars from the head engineer for reducing the concrete effect with the cellulose.

The four inch line conducted the concrete/cellulose mixture into the missile space while the smaller fitting was rigged to an activated carbon particle trap for the escaping air. This wasn't the best set-up, but it would help to decrease the radiation hazard. The operation was proceeding with all due diligence when Buck first saw the muzzle flash, then heard the report. The fight was not yet finished.

Irony—Pend d'Oreille River near Cusick, Washington
0100 Pacific Standard Time

Becker's Team comprised of five other patriots trained by Becker himself moved like ghosts. They crossed the river just after midnight. He gave his men specific instructions and then entered the scrub and willow that lined the upper bank. His instructions had been to move slowly without detection. Then find the sentries and silence them with knife strokes. They watched for three hours before dark from the other side of the river and identified the sentry positions. The only other movement was a truck that slowed along the road at dusk, but it continued north.

Major Sam Becker lay on the ground and recounted his triumphs of the last three days. He had carried the flag of the White American Nation with pride and with surgical efficiency. He thought that after the Nation was in place and his old war wounds began to ache too much to maintain the level of action he now enjoyed, he would take a wife and create some sons and teach them the way of the world. He could see himself with two sons, one on each knee, "Boys, your Daddy was a Major in the Trident War. I personally accounted for 100 non-whites removed from the breeding population." He dreamed that he would extend his hands and show them the scars where his or his opponent's knife had shed blood. "These hands placed over fifty non-whites in the ground," continued Sam's dream. A noise to the left brought him back to the moment.

Sam again heard a rustle, followed by a slight whistling of air. The sound came from the direction of his number two man and sentry position number three. His target was Sentry Two; directly west of his position in a small thicket of Aspen trees about forty yards. He began to inch his way forward. His modified Gilly suit allowed him complete cover without being cumbersome. His phase had shades of dark green, light green and brown in a dry land camouflage pattern. He advanced no faster than one yard per minute. Stealth was about patience he had taught his men. Sam heard himself say, "Men, you can move at night slowly and with patience or you can get killed." He would then conclude with, "Personally, I don't care which you choose. But if your sloppiness causes me injury, I will kill you myself."

Becker heard a rustling sound off to his left in the proximity of Sentry One. That would be his Number Two taking care of business. Sam continued his slow and steady advance. He was nearing the leading edge of the Aspen thicket when he saw movement ahead. He froze. He saw his opponent sitting in a folding camp chair looking slightly to Sam's right. As he continued to observe, the man held his wristwatch up to his face and depressed the button on the case that provided green illumination to see the dial. Sam thought, "What a dumb ass!" It was not only his pleasure, but his duty to remove this subhuman from the breeding pool.

It took Sam a full twenty minutes to move into a position at the left flank of the sentry. Sam walked thought through his attack three times. Then it was time for him to move. Sam moved into a crouch and started to move. Suddenly he stopped forward motion and was lifted upwards. His first thought was that he was exposed and the sentry would see him. Then he felt the restraint on his neck. A thin cable was tightened and would soon cut off blood flow to the brain. His combat training kicked into gear and he pulled his K-Bar and sliced upward with a reverse hold. His thrust was blocked and the knife taken from his hand. He attempted a twisting move, but found that he was now lifted off the ground and off his feet. He was losing consciousness and rotated his head backwards to get a look at his assailant. As his heart pumped the last blood through his carotid arteries his vision started to narrow from the outside. He saw a sight that could not have made his last thought more confused. He saw the front of a night vision goggle with a Hammer and Sickle etched into the faceplate. Just as he succumbed to death, he heard his opponent speak softly in his ear, "Spesnaz."

The Spesnaz commando quietly lowered the dead Major Sam Becker onto the ground. He did not smile; did not move quickly. This commando did not like to kill, but when needed killed efficiently and left his enemy with the name of the man who killed him. The Spesnaz Commando group had been training Air Force officers in survival, evasion, and egress methods at Fairchild Air Force base west of Spokane. When the insurgency across the Pend d'Oreille began, the brass at the base asked them to help out until a S.E.A.L. team or Delta Force could arrive. The older Colonel who commanded this group jokingly responded to the Air Force General, "It will be his and his men's pleasure to kill these rebel Americans." For just a moment the General was not sure what the Colonel had meant.

Later, at the compound, General Stewardt knew that Becker and his men were dead or captured. They were four hours overdue and the spotter on the east shore was also missing. General Stewardt grieved the loss of such a fine weapon, but he had others.

SUNNY DAY—CHAPTER 9

Feet Dry—Snake River Dam near Bliss, Idaho
0740 Pacific Standard Time

Casper was thinking about how his nick name might be prophetic; he might become a ghost soon. He pulled his foot loose from the cable and continued his trip down toward the transformers and tailrace of the dam. He jerked hard and the pain seared through his shoulders and crotch from the tension on his straps. His vision darkened and a black cloth begins to dab-out his sight from the outside inward.

Casper heard a voice, "Son. Trust me. Release your straps." He thought to himself, "So this is what God's voice sounds like." He felt a tug on his left boot, but was afraid to look down. He had heard that when a person lost a limb, it would often return through phantom pain. "Oh my God—I have had a leg fried-off!" thought the pilot. Again the tugging and the voice continued, "Hey, Commander, release your straps—I'll catch you." This time Casper looked down into a large man a mere three feet below him. He released the straps and landed on the concrete.

Casper looked up and around and saw that his canopy was snagged in the cabling for the large transformers and that he was standing next to one of the large units. He looked at the man and began to ask a question, but was beat to vocalization, "The grid was disengaged when we saw the plane crash. It is just standard operating procedure."

Casper was breathing easier, but still had his harness strapped tight to his body. He released the quick release snaps and stepped from his harness. Casper addressed the man, "Do you have a drink of Scotch?" The man led Casper into the dam and shook his head in affirmation.

All Quiet on the Spokane Front—Spokane, Washington
1515 Pacific Standard Time

The Colonel in Gracie's control room grabbed for a chair and stumbled to a sitting position. He finally gained composure and addressed the young Captain in a voice filled with respect and wonder, "Son, I think that will do it. Go ahead and search for any other hostiles. Let me know if you find anything."

The young Captain smiled and said with fighter jock bravado, "Roger, sir!"

The streets of Spokane were filled with burning cars and broken masonry and steel. The mortars played havoc with the older buildings and provided the waiting spark to fulfill the dreams of urban renewal by some city leaders. The scene was one of a city in trouble, but help was on its way. The fire departments and emergency services were activated and would have control by nightfall. Spokane would be back to normal in several weeks.

The Spokane S.W.A.T. team leader had exited the building after being removed from the fire escape when the first Hellfire exploded. As he limped toward the waiting ambulance, he clenched his fist knowing that someone got a clean shot. He would have to make some calls to wives and mothers of his men who would not be coming home. He was sitting a under the Interstate 90 viaduct near Lewis and Clark High School when he turned at a the sound of a large explosion and the top of the building where the bad guys were help up exploded in a towering, billowing fire storm. He clenched his fist again.

Back at Gracie's control room, the Colonel had regained his command stature and questioned the pilot, "Captain, any other disturbances out there?" The Captain replied, "Sir, the battle at the state line is over and Coeur d'Alene is reporting all secure. I don't see any other bad guys in my search. I guess you could say that 'All is Quiet on the Spokane Front'."

The Colonel was ready to give a reprimand for speaking with such familiarity with a superior officer, but chose otherwise, "Yes, son, I guess you could say that." The Colonel ordered, "Take me out to the state line for a look see."

No Mercy—White American Nation Compound near Bunker, Idaho
0800 Pacific Standard Time

The outward sentries had been flushed from their posts and had strategically retreated to the compound perimeter. The compound was crisscrossed with heavy machine guns, rocket-propelled grenades and light automatic weapons. The compound was sealed and secured to keep the leader of the insurrection safe. Reverend-General Stewardt knew that a force could capture the compound, but they would pay dearly. He estimated that with his outside protector force of three hundred men, and his fifty inside protectors, that he could kill at least two thousand attackers on any type of frontal attack. He felt secure.

"Reverend, the night scopes show that the enemy is withdrawing to below the hill and out of sight." said the young man at the controls. The Reverend began to say, "It is God's will, he has sent his angels to drive away the unbelievers, He will exact a..."

The explosion was not impressive as far as sound or visual effect. Each person who was standing within a one-half mile perimeter was knocked-off their feet and those on the ground said that they felt their bones rub together.

The Bunker-buster weapon was the largest ordinance dropped as a conventional weapon except the Daisy-cutter. The weapon entered the compound vertically, penetrated the ground to a depth of twenty feet below the compound and exploded.

There was little left of equipment, body parts or anything tangible or for that matter identifiable. The area was effectively wiped from the face of the Earth.

Ambush—Bangor Submarine Base, Washington
1950 Pacific Standard Time
Men were scattering to various hiding places. The wharf and submarine support area was quickly becoming an armed bunker, rather than an operational facility. Buck looked to his right and the Chief of the Boat was crouched with a pistol in his hand scanning back and forth looking for a target. Buck continued to scan with his own pistol sights for likely targets.

The com link in Buck's ear crackled, "Actual this is god, I have a target acquired; permission to engage."

One of the Ranger team members, known as god, established a superior position and set-up his M107 LRSR (Long Range Sniper Rifle) to control the location. He quickly scanned the wharf and battle area from the top of the crane structure that he chose and found the muzzle flash and the movement. The fellow sniper had found a window of one of the support buildings as his control location. He was well hidden except for the muzzle of the long rifle hanging out the window three or four inches. The enemy sniper was using what appeared to be a 30-06 caliber. This was good because he could rain violence onto his enemy, but his enemy could not reach him.

Buck heard the com link crackle again, "Weapon free; take him out god; this is Actual." Buck appreciated the Ranger commander making the call without hesitation. Ten seconds passed and there was a 'huffing' sound and the wall of a building across the wharf area splintered.

It had taken the Ranger sniper several seconds to settle down to take his shot. His credo 'One Shot—One Kill' was a mainstay of all snipers. He estimated the position of the enemy sniper inside the building and placed the dot of his site on the spot on the wall and settled down for the shot. He fired and viewed through the site after three seconds when his vision came back to full acuity. The barrel was nowhere in site, but he could not confirm the dead body.

"Actual this is god, target prosecuted, but unconfirmed kill. Repeat, unconfirmed kill," reported the Ranger.

This relayed the meaning that he could not confirm a dead, unarmed bad guy to his commander. The com link crackled again and the commander gave additional orders, "Alpha team, enter and sweep the building to the southwest. Listen to instructions from god to locate the sniper location." The com link clicked once. This was a common response to an order.

The com link crackled, "Alpha, this is god; second floor Northeast corner; seven meters from the west wall; copy?" Again the single click of response came over the com link.

Five Ranger commandos move toward the building in a secure formation that reminded Buck of the leap frog tactics when he was a young SEAL team member. The team entered the building and was out of Buck's view. He knew that the team was securing each level of the building and entering each room. The Ranger team would not enter the room in the Hollywood version with loud voices and erupting fire, they would use stealth, practice and precision. Buck found that he was holding his breath and had to focus to breathing.

Thirty seconds passed and then another ten before the com once again crackled, "Actual this is Alpha; target terminated." The Alpha team leader continued, "Boss this guy hid in the ceiling; that is why we did not find him the first sweep."

The Ranger commander responded immediately with orders, "Alpha, Bravo, and Charlie teams sweep buildings again. Use I.R. scopes." Actual continued, "Dragonfly, switch to TBI (thermal body imaging) and sweep the hold; copy?" The unmistakable sound of a helicopter rotor came over the com link, "Roger Actual."

Buck made the decision rapidly as was his reputation. Buck keyed his own com link, "All stations, this is Honcho, return to mission. Get busy." Immediately men returned to their work and guards set about the business of scanning the perimeter. The pumping continued and the extermination work inside the submarine had just concluded.

Buck heard the com link activate with a whirring sound and an impression of an echo in the background, "Honcho, this is Zulu, the Kentucky is secure; all bad guys accounted for and terminated."

Buck responded, "Zulu, remove your men and any bodies. Report to decon with all said; copy?"

Zulu responded, "Confirmed."

Actual broke into the clear with orders, "All stations this is Actual, friendlies exiting the sub. Do not engage."

Buck hoped that the process would soon conclude and he could be relieved of this mess. More and more help was arriving. The decontamination site was in operation and the submarine was starting to sink under the water. Twenty more minutes and the sail of the submarine would be the only area still exposed. It always amazed him that with all of the modern technology, water was still the best at blocking and preventing radiation.

The Chief of the Boat and the Engineering Officer reported to Buck simultaneously. The engineer spoke first, "Sir, we are pretty close to stabilizing the sub. What do we do next?"

The Chief looked at the younger man and smiled. The Chief said, "Hell, son, we drink several cold ones and think about how we can weave this experience into a real sea story." All three men smiled.

Buck simply said, "It is time for clean-up and to count our dead."

Karma—Arco, Idaho
0730 Pacific Standard Time

Chuck Martin was holding his breath again. His eye had left the scope tube and he willed his eyes to peer into the departing jet's bomb bay. His sight moved from the plane to the Idaho National Engineering Laboratory facilities. He knew it was a long shot—literally. He could not stand it any longer. He turned his back to the lab and slumped against the boulder. Impending failure filled his mind; his head slumped.

Round number two had missed the weapons in the bomb bay and had slammed into a fuel transfer line just forward of the bomb bay. The fuel trickle started slowly, but continued at a rate of several kilograms per second. The jet fuel bathed the bomb bay and the remaining weapons. The general vibration of the aircraft caused the round to be dislodged from the fuel line and caused fracture to increase flow. The fuel continued to bathe the underbelly of the F-111. Two seconds had passed since the round found home in the fuel line of the venerable aircraft.

Bravo flight bombardier readied his thumb to depress the microswitch that would release the weapon. The current traveled through the wires connecting the release and arming circuit in the incendiary bomb. As the electrons flowed through the wires to the bomb, a small spark emitted when the plug pulled free from the rack of the bomb bay.

The jet fuel vapors surrounding the plug reached ignition temperature within seven nanoseconds of the spark and the cascade of flame raised the temperature near the weapon to over seven hundred degrees Celsius in 600 nanoseconds after the initial spark. The volatile primer mixture that made the initial explosion possible near the bomb's warhead heated to a critical temperature in 900 nanoseconds after the initial spark. Five nanoseconds after the primer responded to the kinetic energy of the jet fuel fire, the incendiary mixture erupted and the explosive charge reacted violently. The explosion of the fuel-laden F-111 was magnificent.

Chain of Command—Spokane, Washington
2211 Pacific Standard Time

The highest ranking officer in the Columbia War Front with combat background was eighty-six year old, retired Marine Brigadier General Thomas J. Armstrong. He was one of the first African American Generals in the Marine Corps and fought in all of the wars since Korea. He was a crusty, Scotch-drinking exercise fanatic who looked in appearance much like a darker version of Jack Lalane. The Air Force General at Fairchild Air Force Base had his security troops track-down the retired general who was waiting at his house in fatigues for the call. He was briefed on the way to the base.

It was now ten hours since the General took command. He now had eyes and ears in the field. He had secure communication with an Air Force Colonel who had command of the assault in the Spokane battle and broken contact with a Special Forces unit in the river country up North. He also had some mixed signals from the I-90 Bridge and a battle raging near that location. He needed to know what was going on.

He turned to the Colonel who was now his aide and addressed him, "Colonel, I want a big old map and stick pins on that wall. You tell the communications guys to get everything into this space—this is my command post." He swiveled his favorite chair in the Officers Club and looked at the little flags advertising different beer. "What a hell of a way to start a command," he said to no one and everyone at the same time.

Armstrong then gave several other orders, "You two there, I want the police S.W.A.T. team commanders by phone or radio—Now." The two young Air Force officers jumped like they had been scalded. The general thought to himself, "I need a real warrior, not one of these Air Force pukes." In mid thought he turned to the next of a seemingly endless supply of young Air Force officers, "Locate the nearest Marine detachment and I want a Gunnery Sergeant as my aide." He followed this order with a bark, "Move!"

He needed to have fellow Marines around him to feel like he was at war. A Gunnery Sergeant would get this place up and going. Armstrong started identifying targets and remembered what he had been briefed about up at that theme park. One of the scouting teams returned with photos and video of executions and scenes from a concentration camp. He clenched his jaws and placed enough pressure on his teeth that one could imagine pieces of teeth erupting like a volcano from his lips. He vowed to himself that this abomination would be his first organized target. He cursed aloud and a dozen young Air Force officers nearly soiled themselves.

Liberation—Athol, Idaho
0200 Pacific Standard Time

The Marine General had received his requests. In a matter of hours, he had communication with twenty different elements. Some of the troops under his command were police, an R.O.T.C. element, a Spetsnaz unit and a group of irregulars in Coeur d'Alene. There were also some reservists who were leading small raiding units. He also knew that there were some Homeland Security Special Operations detachments that were surrounding, suppressing and suspending operations at the W.A.N. headquarters. His gunny had told him that he watched a short transmission from the television station in Coeur d'Alene that showed attackers hanging from lamp posts.

A man in fatigues with a worn oak leaf insignia on his shoulders said in no uncertain terms, "You who attacked our city—enter Coeur d'Alene at your own risk. Gunny, I want to see that transmission and I want contact with that warrior. I am going to make him a Colonel and use him at the camp," the General shared. The Gunnery Sergeant spun on a dime and went to carry-out his mission. As he left, several Air Force officers trailed him like puppies. The General noticed that the Marine rifleman, in full battle gear, who stood near his chair, grinned. The General addressed the young Marine, "Son, what are you grinning at."

The young Marine snapped to attention and said, "Sir, the Gunny is Hell-on Wheels." The old General just acknowledged the youngster's comment and grinned himself. He thought to himself that only two people were worth their salt in the military. One was a Gunnery Sergeant and the other a Navy Chief Boatswains Mate. Both had salt, hard living and a one track mind when on duty.

He had to use what he had, but the thing he needed most was intelligence about the gulag. He had the blueprints from the park that were on file in Coeur d'Alene and an on-line diagram of the site; however, he wanted real time.

"How long until we get the images from the Predator and the forward observers?" bellowed the General.

The Gunny responded, "Momentarily General." and then turned and gave a look that would curdle milk in the direction of an operator.

Suddenly an image came on the screen. In the upper right margin the letters 'GRACIE' identified the image from the predator stationed at Fairchild Air. The General questioned the operator, "Who the Hell is Gracie?"

"Sir, Gracie is the Predator out of our base here; it is the one that took out the snipers in Spokane." The young man continued, "Sir, it's from George Burns, you know, 'Say Goodnight, Gracie'." The General sat back and smiled. He liked that.

The image began to zoom in and change focus. The image showed the guard towers, the three zones and the work with the dozers. The general caught his breath and issued the order to zoom in on the pits and the dozers. The image sharpened and pixilated then reshaped becoming clear. The General rose from his seat as a chain of cursing erupted from around the room. The image showed a man with a gun shooting a hooded woman in the head. There was also an image of two men swinging a dead body with a hood and throwing it into a trench. The image showed at least forty bodies being covered with soil by a dozer. There were three pits in operation.

A red circle came into the image with a second red pip in the center. The Gunny reacted first, "Tell that Predator Jockey to turn off his targeting system." The General understood the feeling, but they needed information now.

A second image came into clarity in the lower right quadrant; its designation was 'Bravo'. The operator stated, "Sir, Bravo is a scout unit near the camp."

The image shifted and a voice came over the command post speaker system, "Eagle Nest, this is Bravo. Do not respond." The whispered voice continued, "Optical sensors; Clamor in two rows; five towers—automatic and sniper; RPG—estimate twenty;

troops—estimate 200; quality—estimate 20 at grade 5-6, balance at 2-3." The whisper continued, "…have scouted the storm drains—appear un-mined and unguarded; internal power with two redundancy; PKR is 40ph." The message ended with a simple radio request, "confirm receipt with double click—out." The operator in Eagle Nest clicked twice and the image ended and static erupted on the speaker system.

The translated message stated that there were 200 unfriendly troops, 20 of the troops had advanced training and the rest were minimally trained. There were five guard towers with automatic weapons and a sniper rifle. The perimeter of the gulag was mined with two rows of Clamor antipersonnel mines with optical sensors for surveillance. There was a possible stealth approach through the storm drains. The unfriendlies had rocket-propelled grenades and twin electrical generating systems that overlapped in coverage. The last part of the message provided the General with a sense of urgency and for the Gunnery Sergeant to again make the request transfer into a fighting unit in the field. The Prisoner Kill Rate was estimated at 40 individuals per hour.

Two hours later the General had his plan and his units in place or soon to be in place. His assault team consisted of 250 troops. The attack also would unleash a new weapon attached to his three Predator unmanned vehicle. The Lancet Weapon System is a mini rocket ordinance about the size of a large grade school pencil with fins. The Lancet could be configured for individual and general antipersonnel charge, structure charge or concussive charge. While the lancet was not armor piercing, it could shred unarmored structure. Each Predator carried a bundle of fifteen lancets that could be targeted, fired and forgotten. The tracking system allowed for the lancet to communicate with the weapons pod and make corrections. There were two lancets targeted for each guard tower, one with a concussive charge and the other with a structure charge. Four Lancets were targeted for each of the generator sites with structure charges. Four Lancets were targeted through the windows of the suspected command post, two with concussive charges and two with general antipersonnel charges. All of the rest were targeted at unfriendlies in the open and other targets of opportunity.

Thirty commando trained troops were making their way through the storm drains. Some of these troops were Spetsnaz, some reservist and eight 'old men' SEALs who were at Fairchild Survival School as instructors.

The second part of the assault would be through the fence and the mine field. The general had briefed the A-10 pilot himself and had indicated where the Clamor's were placed and where the gunfire from the Vulcan mini-gun needed to be placed.

The pilot looked into the General's eyes and said, "I will plow that area to perdition, sir."

The old General nodded his head and said, "Shoot straight, son."

Everything was set and he had confidence in his troops and his plans. If the Lancets worked, then there would be complete surprise. His commandos had night vision as well as three squads of ten men on the perimeter. He also knew that his men would need the greatest degree of restraint to leave any of the enemy alive. The general tried to remember how many light poles were in the gulag from the images that he saw earlier.

The General made a final decision, keyed his direct microphone for the commander of his commandos and said only two words, "De Guello."

POSTSCRIPT—CHAPTER 10

End of the Nightmare—White American Nation Compound near Bunker, Idaho
0811 Pacific Standard Time

The first troops to approach the crater where the bunker had been only minutes prior were amazed at the lack of identifiable material. The crater was thirty to forty feet deep and had jagged bottom topography. There was an eight to ten foot high berm around the edge of the crater from the ejecta and from the swelling of the ground adjacent to the crater. There was a smell of hot metal and slightly stale and rotting hamburger in the air. If any of the troops were old enough to serve with the big guns of the previous century, the smell was that of cordite.

The Major of the commandos was the highest ranking officer at the bunker facility and quickly instructed his junior officers to establish a perimeter and seek any stragglers or security personnel remaining of the White American Nation. The troops moved quickly and efficiently to secure the area.

The Major was approached by a woman wearing an FBI emblazoned jacket. The Major thought, "Oh crap, here we go with the civilians." His actual thoughts were far less acceptable, but he had learned to think in PG-13 so that he did not slip in front of his kids, wife or commanding officer.

"Major, my name is Special Agent Combs from the Spokane Office. We need to seal this as a crime scene," she addressed the Major. "Our forensics team will want to comb through this mess." The major grunted an acknowledgement concerning the 'mess' part of her comment. Special Agent Combs moved toward the edge of the crater and sucked air through her teeth. She said aloud to the Major, "I don't think that the forensics guys are going to have much luck." The Major moved away from her side and gave orders for several of his men to guard the crater and to protect the evidence.

The Major observed two of his soldiers in a strange posture. They appeared to be talking to the sky. As he came closer to the small group, he heard them say, "Yea, that's right—don't mess with the U.S. Army."

It was then that the Major followed their line of sight and caught the glint of metal. He barked out an order, "Soldiers, attention." The men wheeled around and came erect and the Major quickly said, "At ease." He did not want to make himself or them targets for a sharpshooter lurking on the perimeter. "What the hell were you doing?" he questioned the guiltiest looking of the trio.

"Sir, it is one of our Predators. I bet it has a live feed and my homies will see me back home."

The Major shook his head and addressed the young men, "We just killed a bunch of people. Some were probably women and children. We need to make sure that we act professionally and with respect. Copy?" The young men nodded and went to guard the crater that they now thought of as a grave. The Major gave one final look in the direction of the Predator and then turned to his other duties.

Special agent Combs was still looking at the bottom of the pit and said to herself, "Quick, just, and saved the taxpayers a load of money." She then added her own organic matter to the crater's edge in the form of her own vomit. "That," she thought as she looked at her mess, "is probably the best epitaph for the Reverend Jim Stewardt. She spat out the bile that coated her tongue and left.

Normalcy—Coeur d'Alene, Idaho
1640 Pacific Standard Time

The streets in Coeur d'Alene were quiet, but guarded. Each block seemed to have an organized militia. Guards and alarm signals were in-place and real. Government regained its stature in the form of the County Commissioners. This group of elected public servants sat as policy makers and judges for the short term. It was amazing how effective several people with ultimate authority could act. The 'commissioners' ordered the establishment of a militia, led by the county Sheriff with complete authority of Martial Law. The commissioners were wise in revoking *Posse Commutate* during this emergency and would save the county a great deal in legal fees in years to come. Posse Commutate forbids the use of the military in civil matters under normal situations.

On the fifth day after the attack, the commissioners ordered that the bodies of the White American Nation combatants who were swinging from lamp poles throughout the city be cut down, stacked in the landfill and burned. The commissioners said this was to stop the spread of infection, but insiders knew that they were sending a clear message. The Federal Government sent help to re-establish order, but this aid was refused and Coeur d'Alene slowly returned to normal. For years after the attack, rope adorned the lamp posts. No one said a thing against this clear message.

John Cloud was given the rank of an Under Sheriff in charge of the of the rapid response unit. He had met the Sheriff several times, but was surprised when he got the appointment. He was in charge of 99 other trained militia personnel who insured that the city was secure, operated to inspect suspected W.A.N. locations, vehicles and sympathizers. In addition to the security detail, his group also was in charge of anti-drug activities. The commissioners embarked on a full-fledged anti-drug campaign. Coeur d'Alene had never been so clean.

Hector Rodriguez was still shaken. He heard about battle at the Idaho-Washington state line and volunteered to go help at that site. They were told that the fighting was over, but there was a great need for help for wounded civilians and to track down the W.A.N. members who escaped the fire fight. One of the men in the bus seat next to Hector exclaimed, "Praise Mary, full of grace..." The rest was lost on Hector, because he viewed the killing zone.

Several vehicles were still blazing, but the Post Falls fire department was well in control. What he was not prepared for was the sight of the bodies chained to the metal stands at the bottom edge of the bus. Burned into his memory was the odd angles and fluid nature of the bodies as the hanged slack from their bindings. Hector found his Aunt and Uncle; they were chained to the side of the bus. He also found his cousins; they were inside the bus. Four of his family members were brutally killed; how would he be able to tell his mother?

Hector went to the uniformed man who seemed to be in charge and addressed him, "I want to track down and kill the men who did this."

Sergeant Bavairo looked at the dust-stained tear tracks down the young man's face and placed his hand on Hector's shoulder, looked him deep in the eyes and said, "Amigo your relatives were on the bus?"

Hector looked down and nodded his head. He quickly looked back into the eyes of the Sergeant and said, "I want to make the ones who did this pay with their lives."

The Sergeant nodded affirmation and removed his helmet and then said, "Most are dead and we have the best trackers in the world after the few who escaped. We want those scums alive. I need men to get the bridge open and to get the dead cut off the bus. This bridge needs to be open in two hours."

Hector shook himself erect and told the Sergeant, "I can run any piece of equipment—tell me what you want." The Sergeant and the equipment operator talked of opening the highway and got on with the business of living.

Apocalypse—Athol, Idaho
0500 Pacific Standard Time—evening

The first sound heard inside the gulag was a whoosh. The concussive lancet missiles found their marks in the guard towers and the generator sites. The compound was now dark and the 'claws of the beast' had been removed.

The command squad eased soundlessly into the compound from four different storm drain hatches. The Spetsnaz squad would move to the interrogation and elimination area and secure any prisoners held.

Done Deal—Bangor Submarine Base, Washington
2015 Pacific Standard Time

Things had being going Buck's way for the past thirty minutes. The crews were busily securing the submarine. One crew was building a makeshift cover for the sail. The cover would be constructed from radiation blankets used in routine maintenance on nuclear equipment. He received ten minute reports from the nuclear technician who continuously monitored the radiation. Each time it was better news. The Ranger detachment had secured an ever enlarging perimeter that now included the entire base and a buffer of one mile in all directions. The Blackhawks were orbiting over Hood Canal and were replaced when fuel caused one to leave. The Apache gunships orbited and used their electronics to aid the Ranger detachment in seeking unfriendlies.

Buck had taken the opportunity to visit the warehouse where the enemy was laid on portable cots awaiting N.C.I.S. The Naval Crime Investigation Service would be the lead on this crime along with the F.B.I. and Homeland Security. What struck him most about the group was their ordinary appearance. Each man looked like anyone he had seen on a ship or walking the streets near Pike Place in Seattle. What would cause such men to turn from America?

As Buck left the temporary morgue, he surveyed the clean-up operation. Fewer and fewer personnel were interacting with the submarine. The S.S.B.N. Kentucky and all of her missiles was largely a concrete coffin. While the ship could still float and maneuver, it would wallow like an overloaded party barge on an Arkansas lake. He looked to the far end of the wharf and saw the decontamination unit hard at work. Most of the ambulances were leaving; however, several treated minor wounds and were on standby for anything else that might happen.

The com link sprang to life in Buck's ear, "This is Overlord; approaching Site Omega; Honcho identify your location." This message provided a wealth of information. Overlord was an admiral rank that would take over the incident and more importantly relieve Buck. Site Omega referred to any situation where there was the possibility or actual release of nuclear material or radiation. It was curious to Buck that the folks in the Pentagon could refer to an accident as the 'The End' and still produce nuclear weapons.

Buck keyed his com link and responded, "Overlord, this is Honcho; my location will be mid-wharf 50 meters east of the Kentucky."

The response was immediate, "Honcho, Overlord; E.T.A. three minutes; out." Buck called the Chief of the Boat and the Engineering Officer to give an update to the arriving admiral. Buck keyed his com link again, "Actual this is Honcho; Overlord arriving; proceed my location."

Again military efficiency was demonstrated, "Roger." He saw the Ranger commander exit a small support building on the wharf and head his way.

The sound of approaching vehicles caused all of the personnel to turn toward the east that sloped up to the headlands and the upper portion of the base. He saw several armored vehicles in the command convoy. The foremost of the vehicles was a Humvee with a turret armed with what appeared to be 20mm twin rapid fire heavy machine guns.

In years to come the scenarios played-out in the last several hours would become a virtual reality training program for command grade officers. The virtual reality scenario would include many of the same conditions and at times the names of the personnel involved. The trainee would act in the position of the on-scene commander and be asked to make decisions that Buck had to make in the real situation. The goal of the training exercise was to provide a scenario for command grade officers to understand their limits of authority so that a $5 billion dollar submarine would not be scrapped needlessly.

The Navy determined that officers at the Lieutenant Commander level required this training as this officer grade may be the first on a scene. Buck's decisions were dissected and scrutinized by the

'Monday Morning Quarterbacks' at the Pentagon for years. The training session ended with an admonition from the Chief of Naval Operations about the expectations of Naval Officers in difficult situations. This would become Buck's legacy to the United States Navy. The Pluncket scenario would be utilized to full effect for years.

The first two Humvees and the last two Humvees separated and formed an outward pointing phalanx that allowed the middle Humvee to pull adjacent to Buck and his command and control team. The rear hatch of the Humvee opened and six officers exited from Lieutenant to Rear Admiral. When Buck saw the Rear Admiral he bit through his cigar and found that he was forgetting to breathe. The Rear Admiral walked to where Buck and his team were standing and accepted their salutes. The Admiral turned to the Ranger Commander, "Son, are we secure."

"Sir the area is secured; the 'squids', sorry sir. The navy divers have a port perimeter underwater secure; we have chopper support as well," Actual stated. He continued, "Sir, I would not have allowed salutes if I thought we did not have this completely secure."

Buck had remembered to breathe and was digging the chewed-off piece of cigar out of his mouth. The admiral turned to Buck, "Pluncket, what have you done to my submarine?" The admiral started moving toward what was left of the S.S.B.N. Kentucky. His entire entourage started to move toward the submarine. "Captain, establish a temporary command in one of the dock buildings. Take this entire group. I want a complete engineering, radiation hazard, and situation report from all departments in twenty minutes." The admiral gave commands. The admiral started to walk toward the fallen submarine and spoke to Buck, "Commander shall we go look at your handy work?"

Buck followed the admiral as he made his way to the submarine. The rest of the officers moved toward the nearest building. The Humvees went to appropriate staging locations in front of the building and two departed the wharf area. Buck knew that the two were going to go on a roam and detect of the entire base. When the admiral spoke it jarred Buck back to reality, "Commander, you have been quite busy it appears."

Buck could not believe that this guy was the same one he had knocked on his butt twenty years prior. What kind of cruel fate would make this admiral the same man who sent his men to their death when they both were green young naval officers? The incident had stalled Buck's career, but he had no sour grapes for what he had done.

The inquisition began, "Pluncket, give me the Readers Digest version of the operation."

Buck swallowed, looked the man square in the eyes, and began, "Sir, I arrived to the boomer being held by a hostile party of unknown number and capability. I received the warning that if we tried to board the sub or meet other demands, the team inside would manually set-off the nukes. I determined that they had not yet had time to jury-rig the nukes, so I took action to disable the operation inside and remove the threat. After hulling the submarine and disabling the missile compartment, I filled the compartment with concrete and cellulose fiber. There is a patch over the hole with a four inch valve for mix and a ¾ inch valve for air. The sub is sitting low to allow the water to obstruct radiation."

The admiral interrupted, "What was your last radiation level at the patch, sail, and water surface?"

Buck responded, "The patch is 300% over background, the sail 40% above background and at water level we are par with background."

The admiral continued his questioning, "How many radiation cases with our personnel?"

"Sir, the decontamination team reported that four or five of the sub sailors and Rangers who spent extended time on the boomer had level one exposure. Those men have been evaluated to the base facility for radiation treatment, but the prognosis is excellent."

The admiral moved closer to the submarine. He shook his head. Buck knew what was coming. His only questions to himself is would he get the chance to deck this guy again before they hauled him off to Leavenworth. How many years would it take him to pay the Navy $5 billion dollars?

The admiral spoke again, "Commander, do you believe that you took the appropriate action?"

Buck again looked the man straight in the eyes and responded, "Yes, sir. I stand by my decisions. I believe that I removed threats to the United States and took the action needed at the time." With this statement, Buck retrieved a new cigar and started chewing. The admiral looked at Buck with questions and shook his head.

After what seemed an eternity to Buck, the admiral spoke again, "Pluncket, you did exactly what needed to be done. You probably save the United States a costly terrorist action and saved the lives of perhaps millions of people." The admiral continued, "My report will reflect that you took all of the measures necessary to save lives and acted in the best tradition of the United States Navy." This time the cigar almost slipped out of Buck's gaping mouth.

The admiral changed his tone and appeared to remove himself from his rank, "Buck, you had every right to want answers to why your men died twenty years ago. I couldn't tell you then and I took responsibility as was my duty; however, I can tell you now that I did not order the mission or allow the leak. I was under orders and had already registered my dissatisfaction and concern. I couldn't tell you that then and frankly the fact that I was following orders has no bearing on what I did. I am glad that you were the one who took command of this situation."

Buck took the outstretched hand of the Rear Admiral and followed the handshake with a crisp salute. The admiral again took on the cloak of officialdom and spoke, "Lieutenant Commander Pluncket, I relieve you of this mission."

Again Buck saluted and followed the admiral towards the new command post. Buck thought to himself, "Now I can buy that old salt of a Chief of the Boat the beer we both deserve." Buck walked a little straighter and his forehead showed the horizontal tan stripes of the relaxed furrows that usually creased his face. He reached into his pocket, grasped a new cigar, and unwrapped it before placing it, unlit, into his mouth. He smiled so large that the cigar was in hazard of popping from his mouth.

Aftermath—Southern Idaho
1700 Pacific Standard Time

Southern Idaho was a mess. The fire still raged in the open pit of Ecosafe. Every ten or twenty minutes an explosion caused a flame to erupt and at times a fifty-five gallon barrel would hurdle into the air. The fires would burn for weeks. The lasting effect of this self-imposed toxic incident would not be fully calculated for years to come. Unfortunately, the poisons in the pit were slowly leaching into the arid soil of Southern Idaho. The explosions and fire had cracked the clay liner of the pit and within three weeks benzene, acetone and a plethora of other toxic chemicals would intercept the most mobile and wide-stretching aquifer in the world. Those individuals who breathed the toxic fumes would have serious medical problems for years. Later, a scientist calculated that for every deciliter of fumes inhaled, a reduction of one year in life span would be expected. The reality was much worse.

At the Idaho National Engineering Laboratory things were not that bad. On fourteen low level radioactive containers compromised thirteen had an autofoam system that charged and contained the waste if the barrel were breached. Thirteen of the barrels had been repackaged and the initial radiation reading around the attack site was only five percent above background level. The blast and fire damage was negligible because of the thick concrete construction of the containment building. The only thing that the workers at the INEL site had to worry about was the cloud of toxic smoke on the horizon.

The End of the Beginning—Bob Becker's Residence near Stone Mountain, Georgia
2100 Eastern Standard Time

The men in the room were watching the television coverage intently. Occasionally a grunt or groan would be followed or preceded with a racial epithet or impotent threat. The coverage was amazingly clear, current and uncensored. The bunker attack was from the perspective of the mother aircraft and an unmanned Predator surveillance aircraft that flew close by.

When the large explosion erupted, every man in the smoke-filled, humid room came to his feet. The video coverage went completely white, then black and started to clear after twenty long seconds. During this time there was not a sound in the room except for heavy breathing and the inner workings of intestinal tracts under stress. When the picture became clear, the destruction was immediately apparent. Where the bunker had been was now only a smoking hole in the ground. Many of the men began to curse profusely and the threats against an oppressive government began to flow. One man, however, did not speak nor did he take a seat. Bob Culliman knew only that his brother was dead or captured and any vengeance would be solely his.

Bob walked slowly to the portable coat rack that held all of the robes, jackets and headwear. He donned his robe and began to adjust the different accoutrements. One of his associated came to his side and grasped his shoulder and began a string of cursing and racially-denigrating speech. Bob turned like a cat, grasped the man's throat in a Ranger choke hold and said slowly, two octaves below his normal speaking voice, "Do not give our enemy a name, it gives them worth." Bob slapped the man and released his hold.

The only remaining Culliman avenger spun and addressed the group, "From this time forward we become the tip of the sword. No longer will this organization be a place for drunkenness and general discontent." He allowed a short pause before continuing and made the point of making eye contact with each man. The image on the television was of several dark-skinned soldiers standing in front of the bunker hole celebrating the victory. Bob clenched his jaw. When he continued there was little confusion about who was the de facto leader of the group, "We have a mission tonight, get prepared and muster in front in five minutes." Bob jerked his hood down over his face and moved into the night.

In five minutes the rag, tag group of men assembled in a general muster formation. Bob thought to himself, "How will we get the job done with this group. Oh, well, it is a start." He addressed his men, "Tonight we take the first steps toward returning our country to its correct place in history; tonight we start the revolution." The white robes signifying the Ku Klux Klan slipped into the night to begin the revolution. Bob said under his breath, "We will do it right—no false prophets; it begins!"